A MONSTER'S BEAUTY

EVERNIGHT PUBLISHING ®

www.evernightpublishing.com

SAM CRESCENT

Copyright© 2020

Sam Crescent

Editor: Audrey Bobak

Cover Art: Jay Aheer

ISBN: 978-0-3695-0199-8

ALL RIGHTS RESERVED

WARNING: The unauthorized reproduction or distribution of this copyrighted work is illegal. No part of this book may be used or reproduced electronically or in print without written permission, except in the case of brief quotations embodied in reviews.

This is a work of fiction. All names, characters, and places are fictitious. Any resemblance to actual events, locales, organizations, or persons, living or dead, is entirely coincidental.

A MONSTER'S BEAUTY

SAM CRESCENT

DEDICATION

To all of my wonderful readers. Without you guys, I wouldn't be able to live my dream. Thank you so much for your continued love and support.

A MONSTER'S BEAUTY

A MONSTER'S BEAUTY

In the Arms of Monsters, 3 of 3

Sam Crescent

Copyright © 2020

Chapter One

"This place is nice and cozy. I can see why you like it so much," Reaper said.

Preacher stared at his enemy across the room. He wanted to kill him but he couldn't. In his whole life, he'd never desired anything as much as running the tip of his blade across the man's throat and watching him die. This was fucking unfair and he couldn't believe he didn't see it coming. He should have. Two years Robin had been with this disgusting prick, and yet she was still alive. Sure, she'd been hurt when he found her, but who had she been running to, or running from?

"You better shut your fucking mouth," Bear said.

Neither he nor Bear wanted this man near them, but they had no choice but to accept him into their home. Preacher felt sick to his stomach.

"Or what? You're going to attack me to death with your words? Please, we all know I'm not dying tonight or anytime soon."

A MONSTER'S BEAUTY

"You look happy with yourself," Bishop said.

This was just another cross for Preacher to deal with. Not only did he have Reaper, the fucking leader of Slaves to the Beast, but now he also had his own traitorous son in his home. Two people he wanted to kill more than anything. Things couldn't get any fucking worse. They probably could, but he wasn't going to think about that right now. Nope, as far as he was concerned, they'd already gone fucking bad. Never had he considered himself to be an optimist, but right about now, he was hoping for something, anything to make this all right. There was nothing. The need to kill was strong and building with every passing second, but he kept it at bay. This wasn't the time nor the place to kill all the fuckers here tonight, even if they did deserve it.

"Why shouldn't I be happy? Do you think this has been easy for me?"

"I think you've been pissing yourself laughing at all of us."

"No, not at all. Believe what you want, Bear, but I happen to love your daughter."

"Bullshit," Bear said.

"I need a drink." Preacher left the main sitting room, going into his office and finding the best kind of whiskey money could buy. He didn't even bother with a glass. No, this time, he went straight to the bottle. Downing several large gulps, he closed his eyes, relishing the burn. He couldn't handle this. There was no way Reaper loved Robin. It just couldn't work. It shouldn't work. The son of a bitch was a fucking monster. Robin, though, he knew from experience she had a way of getting under your skin without even trying. She didn't see her charm, or how men wanted to protect her. He did, and even now with the revelation of a baby, he wanted nothing more than to hold her, love her, and tell her it was all going to be all right. He'd find a way.

"I'm sorry," Bishop said.

Now his shitty night got even worse with hearing his son speak. There was a time he did love his son. Bishop was his world. Not enough to marry the kid's mother, but enough to care. All of that had changed in the past few months, and he couldn't believe he hadn't killed him before.

"I suggest you get the fuck out of my sight." He didn't turn around to look at his son. He was holding on by a thread, a really tiny fucking piece of thread.

"I know you're pissed."

This time, he did look at his son and laugh. "You think this is all? I'm a little pissed?" He certainly wasn't drunk. He'd need a hell of a lot more alcohol to even start to numb the shit going on in his brain. Of what he wanted to do to his own flesh and blood. No, Bishop wasn't his son. There was no way a son of his would help his enemy.

"I don't know what you're thinking." Bishop shrugged.

Preacher took another couple of gulps of whiskey. "Let's start with angry. I suggest you go back to your little fuck buddy."

"I'm not fucking Reaper."

"You were supposed to be a Twisted Monster, you little shit. Instead, you gave her to them, and you think a little apology and pretending to give a fuck is going to make it all better?" he asked. "You think that's all it takes?" Where did he go wrong with this kid? What did he do to have all this shit land on him the way it did? He didn't have any answers. Being a dad had always been new to him. He knew deep down he wasn't a good dad, but there were far worse out there.

"I made a mistake."

A MONSTER'S BEAUTY

"No, you royally, totally, and unforgivably fucked up." He didn't know how much more he could control his feelings. Everything was coming at him so fast. Between seeing the baby, the look in Robin's eye, and knowing what Bishop had done, he was ready to wage an all-out war. His hands shook with his need to kill. It had been a long time he'd felt this way. Any other time, he'd just attacked and done whatever he felt was right, no questions asked, but right now, he was far from happy with any of this. He had an overwhelming desire to fuck something up and that anything could be his son. Right now, as he looked at Bishop, he didn't recognize him.

Sure, he'd done his best to raise him and he could openly admit he'd made many mistakes. He never, ever claimed to be a good dad. Never wanted to be a good father. He only wanted to get his son from baby, to toddler, to boy, to teenage, and to adulthood. They were all the important stages, but looking at him now, he wanted to kill him. That feeling may never go away.

"I ... I didn't know this would happen," Bishop said.

"What? You didn't think my biggest enemy wouldn't take her and try to use her against me? How fucking thick and stupid are you? Did you learn anything in school, or were you too busy screwing the girls to even care about that?"

"I'm not stupid."

"Oh, please, you waste so much of your time hating who I am and what I do. You don't think I know about your all-consuming loathing at being known as my son? Do you know why everyone knows you as my son? My boy?"

He gave him a few seconds, hoping Bishop attacked him. All he needed was a single reason to ram his knife into his son's face, or at this point, his fist would be just as good. Anything to make this night worth it all. Bishop didn't move, didn't even make a sound. Even now, he disappointed him. "Because you haven't made a name for yourself. You think anyone gave a shit about Caleb Keats? Hell, no. I had to be the man I am today! Me, no one else. When you start being a man for yourself, you'll learn. Until then, you are royally fucked. The only thing keeping you alive is me. I'm all you've got and what do you do, you shit on me, and take the girl who was nothing but kindness and love to you. You make sure she pays."

Stepping up to his son, he glared at him. "The reason that baby exists is because you were too much of a selfish coward to give a shit. That's why. When you look at her, I hope you see your failings as a friend. She didn't do anything in all of this to deserve your hatred. Me? I can handle everything and anything you throw at me, boy! That's all you are and all you will ever be, a fucking useless boy."

"She fell in love with you," Bishop said. "That's what she did."

Preacher laughed. "You're always the one willing to blame. Everything that happened between us was fucked up. You want to know why she fell for me? You really want to know? I was there for her, Bishop. When she wanted you, or someone, I was the one who stepped up. Do you think it was me she wanted by her side? No, it was you. It would have always been you if you'd stepped up and been a real man. But like always, the only thing you cared about was getting your dick wet, and well, she had grown tired of your bullshit, just like we all did. You were always about yourself, never about her. She saw you a couple of times with the women. She knew you were useless, and she only hoped she was wrong, so wrong, but she wasn't, was she? No, you only care about yourself. It's why when all of this is over, it's going to end very badly for you."

"I need you in there before I tear him apart," Bear said, coming into the room. "He touched my little girl, and I can't ... I need you in there."

"Preacher touched her and you got no problem with that," Bishop said.

Bear walked into the room, a smile on his face. "What did you say to me?"

"You heard me," Bishop said.

Preacher didn't stop Bear as he slammed his fist into Bishop's face. "You should be grateful you're still standing. I would take my sweet time with you, make you bleed long before I give you a chance to make it up to me. You fucked this club. You turned on Preacher, but as far as I'm concerned, you caused my baby girl nothing but pain. You even let me believe that I was right in thinking she died. Not anymore. The moment his protection of you ceases, I'm having your ass, and it's never going to see daylight again."

Keeping hold of his whiskey, Preacher returned to his sitting room to find Reaper with this big old smile on his face, sitting on his sofa and sinking into the seat. There was no reason for him to stop whatever Bear had been saying to Bishop. His son was on borrowed time.

"You're loving this, aren't you?" There was no denying the gloating look on Reaper's face as he watched what he'd caused to unfold.

"What's not to love?" Reaper asked. "Do you have any idea how hard it was to watch the way you guys were fucking up? Bethany wants her mother and I need her as well. We'd become one nice, big, happy family."

"A big family? You have one kid." He wasn't going to acknowledge that Robin had called their girl

Bethany. She'd wanted to call their child Bethany, the one she'd lost. No, he couldn't go there. Not right now.

"What, you think I can't have many more? I know what Robin feels like riding my dick, I know how she tastes, and those sweet little moans she makes when you touch a part of her just right."

Everything he was saying only served to fuel Preacher's anger. "You got what you came here to do. Leave."

"No, I'm not leaving, and you and I both know you're not going to kill me. Not while Robin wants me alive. I'm her baby's father and you can't take away the fact she's in love with me." Reaper released a large sigh. "This feels good. I can see what you love about the place. It's very homey. The perfect place to raise a child. I've missed her in my arms, you know. Robin. She does love it when you hold her. She smells so much like lemons, but I guess both of you know that, huh? You and you, you've held her in her sleep."

Bishop had returned to the room but Preacher ignored him. Reaper wanted to get a reaction out of him, and so far, he'd already played to his ways. Not anymore.

"I fucked her on that sofa," Preacher said.

The smile on Reaper's face dropped. Two could play this game. This made him feel at least a little happier.

"She screamed my name as I drove inside her, making her come over and over. She loves it when you suck on those big nipples of hers." He ran his tongue across his lip and smiled. "She does love to feel a tongue on her pussy. It's one of her favorite things." Preacher had no real desire to thrust his time with Robin in front of Reaper, but if the bastard was insistent on constantly bringing it up, then he was going to fight back.

"I don't need to hear this. I know what we had."

"Yeah, well, she's had plenty from me since then, and seeing as she didn't leave with you, I'd say it's safe to say Robin's mine." Preacher sipped his whiskey.

"Yeah, well, that was all before I took her," Reaper said.

"I wasn't talking about before you kidnapped her, asshole. I was talking just the other day." He stared at his enemy. "You want to paint whatever you think was going on between the two of you as some kind of love connection. It wasn't. You kidnapped her. You had no intention of falling in love with her. All you wanted to do was use her against me. There's no way that is any kind of love."

Reaper stood up. "And now I've got a kid with her, which is more than you can say."

"And I can quite easily look after her. You're not needed." He didn't allow Reaper's words to bring up that one night where he held Robin through the pain of her miscarriage. This bastard didn't know what it was like to hear her screams and do nothing to help her. He didn't know what love was.

"I'm not leaving her behind," Reaper said.

Preacher stared at Reaper. He couldn't help it, he burst out laughing. "Oh, my fucking God, you have got to be kidding me right now." He'd hated Reaper for as long as he could remember. They had never been friends.

"I'm almost afraid to ask right now," Bear said. "I've heard enough of dicks and orgasms to last me a lifetime. I don't know if I can stomach much more and everything coming out of this fucker's mouth is bullshit."

"You're in love with her, aren't you?" Preacher glared at Reaper. He didn't want to believe it was true.

"No, that's not possible," Bishop said. "He took her and intended to use her against you, against all of us."

"Don't even for a second try to get out of your part you played in this, Bishop. If it hadn't been for you, I wouldn't have been able to take her so easily." Reaper chuckled.

"Yeah, and it seems the joke is on all of us, isn't it? You fell in love with her," Preacher said.

"What I feel for her is none of your business. I came here so Bethany could see her mother. I risked the chance of you killing me for this."

"Does it bother you?" Preacher asked.

"Does what bother me?" For the first time since they'd seen him, Reaper looked annoyed, frustrated even.

"You took her to cause me pain. To make my life a misery and instead, you fell for her hard. I wonder what that must feel like to you," he said. Preacher knew what it was like to fall for Robin. He'd gone hard, fast, and he hadn't even seen it coming, but it had happened, and now there was no way for him to stop these feelings. They were part of him, and he felt utterly consumed by them. He would do anything for Robin, even entertain his enemy.

"It doesn't matter, does it?" Reaper said. "I've still got Bethany. I've got more with Robin than you have."

"And she's settled now in bed, and you don't need to keep on doing this. Competing with each other," Robin said, drawing their attention.

Preacher looked at Robin. She appeared pale as if she was a little sick. Her gaze moved from Reaper to Preacher, then back again. She nibbled on her lip, nervousness clear on her expression. For the longest time, she didn't speak, only looked. The tension in the air mounted as he waited for whatever she was going to say, only for nothing to happen.

"I need a drink." She walked away and Preacher

A MONSTER'S BEAUTY

went after her. He didn't want this to overwhelm her, or for her to think he couldn't handle this. She was his and no matter what happened between her and Reaper, he'd support her, he'd be there for her.

Could you stay with her if she fell in love with him and wants to go back to him?

The very thought made him feel sick to his stomach. He didn't know if he'd ever be able to handle that kind of pain.

No, he wouldn't think about it, not yet. He'd only deal with that bullshit when it actually happened, if it ever did.

Reaper followed directly behind him. Robin didn't go to his office for a hard drink of liquor. She went to the kitchen, opening up the fridge and taking out a bottle of water. This wasn't what he expected.

"You know, no one would hold it against you if you had a drink," Preacher said, offering her the bottle. He'd hold her for as long as she needed him.

She shook her head. "No, I don't want to drink. I just, I need a minute. I haven't wanted a drink since Milly did what she did." She wrinkled her nose. "Wow, don't you wish there are some memories you can always forget." She looked toward Preacher. "You know the ones."

He nodded.

She ran fingers through her hair. "I'm getting a headache." She covered her face with her hands, and he watched her take several deep breaths.

"I'm here," Preacher said.

"You need to go and lie down?" Reaper asked.

"No. A lot has happened and right now, three worlds are colliding together. I don't have to go to sleep."

"Three?" Bishop asked.

She dropped her hands and glared at Bishop. "Why are you still here? You're not even wanted here."

"I want to help," he said.

This time, Robin was the one to laugh. "Now you want to? You want to help me? Really? After everything you've done, you think I want your help? Do you think I want anything from you?"

"Robin, please," Bishop said.

"The only reason you could possibly want my help right now is because a whole bunch of people want to kill you. Like always, you're only thinking about yourself. You're all you ever care about. I feel sorry for the woman who thinks she can make you a better man because it isn't ever going to happen. I don't want you dead. I don't want to live with that on my conscience … I can't think right now, and I don't want you near me. You're the last person I ever want. Every single time I've needed a best friend, all you've ever done is screw me over. I've come to see, Bishop, screwing me over is what you do best. It's what you always do, and you enjoy it."

"Robin…"

"I don't want you here." She looked at Preacher. "I know it's your house, but…"

"Get out," Preacher said. "You're free to leave. My men won't kill you. But Bishop, if you leave town, there's no guarantee."

Bishop didn't move and she stared at him. Preacher watched them. There was an unspoken message between them. One he didn't know.

They'd been friends forever. There was nothing he could do to take it away.

"I'm not going to change my mind. You can't give me puppy dog eyes anymore. We're done here, Bishop. I'm not even going to extend friendship to you. Not anymore."

A MONSTER'S BEAUTY

Bishop nodded his head, turned on his heel, and left. He slammed the door behind him and Robin laughed. "He's always the one to be dramatic."

She looked at Preacher. "We need to talk."

"Forgive me, baby, but I'm not allowing you to be alone with him." Reaper just had to impart his thoughts, even if they weren't required.

In his mind, Preacher thought about taking out a gun and shooting him in the head.

"Reaper, I've been alone with him for nearly a year. I need to talk to him and I don't care if you like it. After everything, it's the least you could do and I'm not asking for permission. Neither of you ever do that, do you? Ask for permission from anyone. You just do whatever the hell you want. Well, I'm going to start taking advice from both of you. It doesn't seem to be doing either you any trouble." She walked out the back door, heading onto his porch, leaving him alone with Reaper.

Reaper grabbed his arm. "This doesn't mean anything."

Preacher slammed his head against the kitchen counter. "No, it doesn't, but if you ever touch me again, I will fuck you up, Robin or not. You're breathing because she wants you to. The moment you cross any line and you lose that tiny thread of connection with her, your ass is as good as dead."

He left his kitchen. The desire to slam his own kitchen door was strong, but he decided against it. Instead, he closed it silently and found Robin sitting in the cold, looking out into the night. He could and would always be the bigger man.

The last few hours had been … fucked up. There was no other way to describe it. No way he could think to describe what had happened.

Robin had gotten her memory back. This, for Preacher, had been great. She remembered them, their time together, what drew them closer. Then the meet-up with Bishop, followed by the harsh reality of her truth. It must have been hard for her. She hadn't fallen apart, but he knew anything could happen to spiral her down a pit of despair.

Before Reaper had shown up with Bethany, Robin had told him everything. Bethany's birth, her feelings for Reaper, even her acceptance of staying with the prick. All of it had come spilling out.

He couldn't hate her though. Not after what she'd gone through. Sure, he'd hated hearing her share her feelings. How she'd finally given up hope and just tried to make the best of a bad situation. The last thing he ever wanted her to feel or do was to have to make do. She was better than that, but he hadn't been in her situation. He didn't know what she went to or why she finally decided to give up.

"Do you want to hurt me?" Robin asked.

He heard the sob within her voice and he took the seat beside her, pulling her into his arms, holding her as tightly as he could without hurting her. "I could never hurt you."

"I'm a slut."

"You're not."

"I was with another man, Preacher. We have a child together. Now I'm so confused. I hate Bishop. I want him to suffer. I hate myself."

"You should never hate yourself." He stroked her hair.

"How can I not? I was weak."

"You're not weak."

"If Bishop hadn't done what he did, this could've been me and you. I hate him so much."

"Just say the word and it's done. I'll kill him." He was serious. It was like he felt her acute pain.

"But what if I miss him? I can't have his death on my conscience. I just ... can't. Damn it. Don't get me wrong, I do want to kill him, but not like this. I don't want to ever allow him to make me feel any kind of guilt."

"You won't. His death wouldn't be caused by you."

"He's your son," she said.

"No son of mine would do what he did." As far as he was concerned, Bishop wasn't his. He'd already killed him in his own mind.

"He was upset."

"And if that was the argument against all men who made a mistake, you think the courts would be needed? Slap him on the wrist? He fucked up, made a mistake. All is forgiven."

"You know I don't mean that."

"I want you to understand that because of him, you were taken. I saw the picture of you, Robin. Before all of this with Bethany, it wasn't nice and loving. Don't ever forget this started out as a kidnapping. He took you because of me. He hates me. Reaper hurt you. He tortured you, raped you, and yet, you still fell in love with him. What kind of fucked-up mess did he do to you?"

"I don't ... I know you're angry."

He held her even tighter. "No, I'm not angry, baby. I'm far from angry." He kept his arms around her. "If you want Bishop gone, all you have to do is say the word. All I want to do is make this better for you."

"Not yet. I can't make that decision about Bishop. You shouldn't be making it better for me. I should suffer."

"Do you love him?" Preacher asked.

"I don't know. I think so. I'm so confused right now."

"Then don't think about it. Not now. Not ever. I'm not going to force you to make a decision."

She took a deep breath. "I do love you, Preacher. That I know without a doubt."

"I know. I know." He kissed the top of her head. She loved him and he'd never question her about that. It was what she felt for Reaper that he wanted to know. Why she didn't want Reaper dead, and why he was right now standing at the back door, looking at them. He wanted to rub Reaper's nose in the fact he was holding her, but he didn't. Instead, he basked in having her in his arms and knowing when it came to this woman, he would do whatever she needed him to do and not question why. He trusted her, had faith in her, and there was no one else in his world he wanted more. Even if she still hadn't given him the all clear to hurt the bastard who had taken her from him. Whatever her reasoning, he'd wait until she was ready.

****

Robin was always told falling in love would be so easy. At least the storybooks and the movies showed her that. People around her gave her a hint. Whenever she looked at her parents, she honestly didn't believe in love or love at first sight. Her parents had nothing but hatred between them. There was no joy, no love, just an equal measure of detest for one another. Love, if it happened, was supposed to be easy, right? Two people would meet each other, feelings were explored, love would develop, and it would just be a perfect story of being together. Then her life happened. Bishop, Preacher, Reaper, all the men, and now she was so confused.

Pulling away from Preacher, she knew she had to

stand on her own two feet, now more than ever before. This wasn't the time for her to fall. She had to be strong.

"I gave birth to her in a car," she said. She started to laugh. "Reaper was showing me this house. He was willing to settle down. I was scared when it came to Bethany. I didn't think constantly being on the move was a good idea. I had gotten sick during one of our moves, and I nearly died," she said.

Preacher took her hand. "I know you want some space right now, but I need to hold you. It'll stop me going in there and killing him dead."

She smiled. Her hands were cold and his were large. They still had a way of making her feel safe, secure, and warm. "I know this is hard for you."

"Nah, this is a piece of cake for me. I'm concerned about how you're dealing with all of this," he said. "You got to remember, not so long ago, you didn't even know your name."

"That would have been a lot easier, wouldn't it?" She laughed, but it was a forced sound. "I'm dealing. It's all I can do." She shrugged. "Reaper helped me give birth to our daughter. I held her in my arms and he drove us back to the hospital. We didn't use our names, but I registered Bethany there. She was so healthy."

"She looked beautiful," Preacher said. "Did you put her in the nursery?"

"Yes."

"Can I go and see her?" Preacher asked.

"You'd like that?"

"It seems when it comes to you, Robin, I don't really think straight. I'd like to go and see your daughter. I might be able to understand why you don't want me to hurt the man who took you." He got to his feet and she followed him.

Turning around, she was hit by guilt once again.

Reaper stood watching her, his gaze questioning. This was so fucking hard. Why couldn't she go back to when it was easier for her, when she hated Reaper more than anything?

From the moment she'd gotten her memory back, each second had been a harsh bombardment of reality she couldn't deal with. But she had to. Her mother once told her she was weak, that she was nothing. That was laughable. It wasn't one time. No, her mother liked to tell her repeatedly what a disappointment and a failure she was. Nothing she ever did was good enough or right. For the longest time, she'd believed her, and yet, she'd gone through a lot already and was still standing.

Taking a deep breath, she stepped inside the house where Reaper was waiting. He looked … expectant. She didn't know if that was the right way to describe him.

"Robin," he said. He made no move to touch her or to reach out but there was something in his eyes, like he expected her to do something. Maybe she was overreacting here. Whatever the reason, she didn't like it.

"I … I'm showing Preacher Bethany," she said.

"He'll hurt her."

"No, he won't."

"He hates me and he'll hurt my daughter."

"Preacher won't do any such thing. He hurts the people who deserve it, not the innocent. If I'm still walking and breathing, then Bethany is fine." There was no way Preacher would ever harm their daughter. He was many things, but a monster to babies wasn't it. Sure, he wanted to kill Bishop, but his son was neither a baby, nor innocent.

"I would never hurt you, Robin," Preacher said. "And I won't harm a defenseless child, no matter the father. I left O'Klaren's children alone, didn't I?"

"Let's not argue," she said, holding her hands up. "This won't do any of us any good. Please, I need us all to stay focused."

"If he's going, I'm going."

"This is his house, Reaper. You know he's the one who's going to make all the rules, not us."

"And he knows I'm not going anywhere," Reaper said.

"This is fine," Preacher said. "I don't mind him being here so long as he knows his place, which is far the fuck away from me."

"I don't want Bethany to be caught up in this. This is my fault," she said, looking between the two men she'd fallen for. Neither man deserved what she'd given them. They were both there, waiting for her to make a decision, one she couldn't make.

There was no doubt in her mind what this all meant.

One day very soon, she was going to have to make a choice. A choice between these two men, but right now, she didn't have a clue how she was ever going to be able to pick. "Can we please go and see her?" That choice wasn't needed today.

She didn't wait for anyone to respond. Turning toward the staircase, she paused, knowing her father was waiting in the sitting room. "A moment," she said.

Leaving the two men by the stairs, hoping they wouldn't kill each other but not putting it past them, she found her father in the sitting room, nursing a bottle of water.

"I figured you'd want a stiff drink."

"I don't drink anymore and I haven't for some time." He sipped at his bottle of water. "At least I try not to. Taking it one day at a time."

"I'm taking Preacher to see Bethany. Would you

like to see her?"

"No," he said.

"Oh."

"Look, I know right now you're happy with everything. You've gotten to see your daughter and your memories have returned. But him being here, it's not going to end well, and you're a fool if you think there's any chance this will work."

She nodded. "I don't know what to do, Dad. I'm trying to make the right decisions here. I don't want to hurt anyone."

"Don't make the right decision for everyone, make the final decision, and you know what I mean. No matter which way you look at his, sweetheart, someone is going to get hurt. Now, one person out there deserves it. Bishop as well. The other, well, he was the one who wouldn't stop looking for you. Who wouldn't give up on you no matter what."

"I know."

"I hope you make the right decision."

"You're really not going to come and see her? She's your granddaughter, and she didn't do nothing wrong."

"I know. I know, but after tonight, I just need some space. I'm not like Preacher. I don't trust myself."

"Oh, okay." It hurt knowing her father wanted nothing to do with her little girl, but she couldn't judge him, not after everything. While she'd been taken, he'd seen everything Preacher had gone through, and she could only imagine the pain he'd witnessed.

She stepped back and returned to find Reaper and Preacher staring off at each other. Sick to her stomach, she only smiled at them. "I'm sorry to keep you guys waiting." She didn't anticipate a response and she rushed upstairs into the nursery.

A MONSTER'S BEAUTY

On entering, she felt a wave of sadness that always struck her. This was supposed to be her and Preacher's baby's room. Was she making a mistake bringing Bethany here? Was this cruel of her, expecting Preacher to just allow another man's child to sleep in this very room? The same room he helped her to decorate and build. Everything was all going so crazy, and she didn't know what the hell to do anymore. Nothing made any kind of real sense to her.

Now with her memories back, the old pain and regret flooded her. Stepping up to the crib, she tried to push down her feelings. She loved Bethany. There was a love she didn't know could even exist as she stared at her innocent child, but it was there, simmering beneath the surface. She stroked her sleeping daughter's cheek.

She'd have loved for Bethany to wake up, to scream, to relieve the tension, but nothing.

"She's beautiful," Preacher said, stepping up beside the crib. "I ... I bet it's been tough for her to not have her mother with her."

"It has, but I consoled her." Reaper's voice permeated the room.

Preacher gritted his teeth and all she wanted to do was reach out, hold his hands, and tell him it was going to be okay, but how the fuck could she do that when she didn't have a clue how to deal with all of the other chaos going on in her head? Not only had her memories returned but so had this need as well. The love of both men, and that she wished she had never returned. She saw the hatred between them. Knew deep in her heart there was only one man she could be with. Bear was right. Someone was going to get hurt. If she picked Reaper, she'd always wonder about Preacher. She was torn from him even before they had a chance to be together. If she picked Preacher, Reaper's death wouldn't be soon after.

To many, this was an easy decision, but to Robin, it wasn't.

When she gave birth to Bethany, she truly believed she'd never be near or see Preacher again. She never for a second thought she'd fall right back in love with him, desperate for his touch and his love.

Now, she also held that love for Reaper. Yes, there were the bad memories, of course there were, but this, it wasn't right.

"Would you like to hold her?" Robin asked.

"When she's awake, maybe. Excuse me."

Preacher left the room. She listened as he talked to her father downstairs and flinched as the door to the house closed.

This was all a little too much for all of them.

Tears filled her eyes. The slamming of the door had unnerved her daughter. Humming softly to her, she made sure she felt safe.

Reaper stepped forward. He put his hands on her hips and her first instinct was to pull away but she didn't.

"You were at the supermarket," she said.

"I knew they were planning something for your birthday. I've kept a close eye on you. As much as I could without being caught."

"Why didn't you say anything?"

"I didn't know if seeing Bethany would help you to remember. I knew you needed to have some catalyst."

"It didn't." She blew out a breath. No, all of her memories returned when she'd stepped inside Bishop's room. Of all the places for her to be reminded of everything that happened. At least it explained her nerves about being around Bishop.

"I know. Don't get me wrong, I was hoping for a little of that love action to help us. You know, the shit you like reading about. Guy meets girl and all of that."

"Don't cuss, please."

"You think that's the worst Bethany is going to hear? You grew up in this world, Robin."

"She doesn't need you. You said that."

"I said a lot of things, like you'd be safe, but we both know you weren't."

She turned toward Reaper and he groaned. "Shit, baby, don't cry, please."

She pulled away from him. "It's fine."

"It's not fine. I'm not going to hurt you."

"I know that." She walked over to the window.

Preacher's bike was gone. He'd left without another word. This was all a little too much for him. "You know he could have killed you today."

"I know, but I also know he loves you as much as I do, and he won't do anything to make you sad or angry. It's the way of the world. Love wins over all."

"Does it? I'm starting to doubt that."

"You told me that all it takes is having some faith in others. It's why I came back here, Robin. To show you I have faith in you, in us."

He had faith in her? Love. The one feeling that should make all others go away. Love should be easy. She no longer believed that. If love won and if it was easy, then she wouldn't be in this predicament. She released a yawn and realized how tired she was. "I need to get some sleep. I don't know how long she's going to be out for."

"Bethany sleeps well. She's never a bother. We've been lucky with her."

"Did you have other women taking care of her?"

"No, I took care of her. She's my girl, and you know there's no one else I'd trust with her safety. I knew you wouldn't be happy with anyone else taking care of her."

"Thank you."

"I'd never replace you, Robin. You know that."

"I'm sorry. I guess I'm really tired. Please don't be angry with me. A lot has happened tonight."

"It's impossible to be angry with you."

She reached out to touch his cheek and hesitated.

Reaper cursed, grabbed her shirt, and pulled her in close. She let out a moan as he took possession of her lips in a searing kiss.

It was the first time they'd kissed in so long. At first, it felt awkward. This man had been part of her other life and now, he was there kissing her, loving her, and it was just a little too much, but she responded.

Her body ... didn't. There was something missing. She cupped his cheek and pulled away. This was Preacher's house. Reaper, her feelings for him, it wasn't ... right. She didn't know what was suddenly missing.

You're no longer a captive, and he's no longer in charge. You're safe now, and you don't have to make sacrifices to live or to be happy.

"Fuck, I've missed you."

"I'm going to go say goodnight to my dad. You can sleep in Bishop's old room or on the sofa. I don't know where else you'd stay."

"I'll take the sofa. I'm not sleeping in that guy's cum dump."

She couldn't help but chuckle. "Goodnight."

"Goodnight. I'm just going to watch her, make sure she is settled."

Robin nodded. She went to her room, changed into a pair of pajamas, and went in search of her father. She found him passed out in the chair. The bottle of water half-empty beside him.

She grabbed the blanket and threw it over him.

He opened his eyes.

"Sorry, I didn't mean to wake you."

"I'm not going to sleep. Just relaxing."

"I'm heading to bed."

"Do you have any idea what you're doing, Robin?"

"No, I don't."

"You need to start making a decision about this."

"Dad, please."

"No, Preacher and Reaper can pander to your needs, but I won't. That little girl up there can't be pulled between those two men."

The tears she'd been holding in finally decided to fall. "I can't do this. Not right now."

"Then do it soon. Don't string them along. You're not the kind of woman to do it, so don't start now."

"Dad, do you even know me? Do you even know what I went through?"

"Right now, I really don't care. All I know is Preacher nearly tore the club apart trying to find you and then he did exactly the same trying to find his rat of a son and that asshole upstairs. I don't have time to care about what happened to you."

"I'm your daughter."

"And you know what it means to be part of the club."

"Yeah, I know what it means. Isn't that why Mom ended up being killed? She couldn't handle being with you so she turned on you and the club?"

Bear laughed. "You know that anger you're feeling right now, direct it at someone who gives a fuck. I get that you've had it hard, believe me, I do. But don't for a second think your life isn't expendable."

"Wow, I get my memories back and all of a sudden, I'm nothing."

"Oh, my daughter is something. I love her more than anything, but you see, my Robin, she never would've had a kid with the enemy. She's better than that. Right now, all I see is the whore who fathered a bastard's child."

"Actually," Reaper said, "you better be careful how you speak to my wife."

Robin closed her eyes. "Wife?"

"Yeah. Bishop's hatred of you and the entire club, it drove him to make one other decision. Bishop and Robin haven't been married for some time now. So, I took care of that little deed. She and I are very much married. Also, I might want to warn you Robin didn't have a choice. I know you've got a problem with me, but your daughter isn't a whore. The only reason you're still sitting there feeling all superior is because I know my wife wouldn't like me to kill you, but don't push me. There's only so much I'm willing to have Robin put up with, and you, my friend, are holding on by a thin fucking thread. Bishop is the cause of all of this, not Robin. You keep those threats of yours to yourself, otherwise, you and I are going to have a serious problem."

"I need some air," Bear said.

She didn't watch him leave. The moment she heard the door slam, she opened her eyes and Reaper was there.

"I guess you didn't get to that little detail."

She shook her head.

"I'm sorry."

"It doesn't matter. I … I've got to go to bed." She turned on her heel, about to leave the room.

"I can take you away from all this. You don't

have to set foot or be anywhere near Preacher and his club. They don't deserve you. You certainly don't need to listen to what they say to you. You're not a whore, never have been."

She turned toward him and waited.

"You're better than this," he said. "You're better than all of this."

"You never gave up your club or what you did, not even after I gave birth to Bethany. It's why I ended up back here, broken, hurt, and tortured. Do you have any idea what those men … did to me?" She pressed her lips together and waited.

"Robin."

She took a step back. "I don't…" She stopped needing a minute, or ten. "I need to get some sleep. It's been a really long day."

Without looking back at him, she climbed the stairs and went straight to her bedroom rather than the one she'd been sharing with Preacher. It was now wrong to share a bed with him. If she climbed into his bed, would Reaper demand the same? It was confusing, and all she wanted to do was fall asleep. To be somewhere where her troubles didn't exist. Where she didn't have to make choices and decisions or remember what had once been.

After grabbing the spare pillow, she placed it over her face and sobbed.

Chapter Two

"I didn't expect to see you here," Dog said.

Preacher removed his leather cut and wrapped some bandages around his fists, flexing them. "Whoever you've got lined up tonight, change it. I'm going on."

"Seriously? You're going to come here and tell me how to work my men and my business?"

"Most of them have a death wish. It's why they come here in the first place. Don't give me all that bullshit about how they need the money and stuff."

"Preacher, I hate to break it to you, but you and I have a working relationship. Your boys, they don't like me."

"I don't give a fuck what it is they like or don't like. I know what I want you to do. Now, organize for me to go on there."

"And if you die?"

"It's a decision I make."

"This is fucked up."

"Listen to me, Dog, I'm not asking for your permission. What I'm telling you right now is if I don't go out there and hurt or kill, then I'm going home and murder the bastard who raped my woman and impregnated her with his kid, then kill my son who allowed it all to happen."

Dog paused. "Wait a second, these people aren't dead already?"

"I've got a deal with the fucking devil and I can't kill them, not yet. It is all about timing."

"Why the hell not?

Preacher gritted his teeth. "Do you want to be on my list? I've got no problem putting you there."

"You really are in an awfully shitty mood."

"Yeah, well, you haven't been me for the last

twenty-four hours. Believe me, if you had, you'd be wanting to fight as well."

"You do know none of these fights are guaranteed. You could die out there. I can't stop that."

"I'm not wanting to party, if that's what you're getting at. I want to fight. This isn't for show. I've got to do something, and seeing as my hands are tied right now, this is all I've got."

"Wait. All of this because of the love of a woman?"

"Yeah, speaking of the love of a woman, Robin has her memories back. I'm thinking Sunday, two o'clock for the dinner I promised you. Don't worry, the other guy claiming to love her is already there. Welcome to my fucked-up life."

Dog stared at him and suddenly started to smile. "Your life is sounding crazier than I ever imagined. Count me in. I love family drama as much as the next dick. I've got to see what all of this is about. If you die today, I will hunt and kill Reaper for you in your place, just so you know."

"Why?" Preacher asked.

"It's what friends are for and last time I checked, I'm not in love with this woman who seems to have everyone's dicks locked up so fucking tight. You know, it's easier to fuck whores. They know the score. There's no attachment. They're there for one simple purpose in life and that's to take dick however we choose."

"Said like a man who hasn't found the right woman. Believe me, when you do, you'll be surprised at the lengths you'd go to just to be with them."

"I'm not the one on a suicide mission because of a woman. I'm very much sane, which is a nice feeling. It's nice not being the crazy one for a change. How about that?"

He didn't wait around to see what else Dog had to say. He walked right into the thick of the ring and the crowd was told there would be a change of plans.

Preacher watched and waited as he saw his opponent hesitate. He wanted the prick to hesitate, to be nervous. They all should be nervous around him. He was a fucking killer. For too long, he'd been holding back, and he was no longer going to be on a leash. They would get the real monster tonight.

The bell rang and he didn't bother to do the whole circle and foreplay some fighters seemed desperate to act out. He was more interested in killing.

He slammed his fists against the guy's stomach, charging at him, pushing him to the edge of the circle, and hitting his face. He took one to the face himself but Preacher didn't stop. In the back of his mind, all he saw was Reaper. The way he stood holding Bethany as if it made him better because the bastard was able to have a kid with her, and then he heard the distinctive sound of Robin's screams. Her cries and begging for him to stop her from losing their baby, but he couldn't help nor could he stop what happened. She lost the baby in his arms, and he had to deal with the anger, the hatred, the loathing all over again. Where Reaper had succeeded, he'd failed big time. Now he had to deal with the consequences of that, and it angered him, frustrated him.

Within a matter of minutes, his opponent was dead. A snap of the neck ended it, and the crowd roared for more. It hadn't helped him with his thirst, his bloodlust. No, this was just the start.

Preacher wasn't done and out came the next man. This one was more energetic and he got several punches in. The blows fell off him because they didn't hurt. It was impossible to hurt him as the pain he already felt was indescribable.

A MONSTER'S BEAUTY

Robin had told him the truth. Expressed her concern about her own feelings. She'd been open and honest with him, which was all he'd asked, but knowing she had feelings for the sick bastard, it ... angered him. How could she ever fall for that monster?

He wanted to scream at her.

You're calling him sick?

What about you?

Didn't she put up with you because of what you did?

I was drunk.

Yeah, and you liked knowing you knocked her up. Stop being all self-righteous. You're not the victim here.

His opponent became nothing but a bloody mess as he kept punching his face until nothing was visible and he was dead. Robin, in all things, was the victim and he had to remember that. There was nothing about this that he could blame her for, not really.

Dog organized the next man and of course, it all started again. Preacher was a pro at this kind of fighting. He knew what his body could take and how much strength he needed to land the right punch to get the job done. With each blow, he forced down his opponents, relishing the crunch and destruction of bone. The body was a frail thing. The right knuckle in the right place and it was all over.

And you're going to ignore it all over again, aren't you?

Yes, it was a big, fat mistake fucking Robin, or should I say, date rape? You didn't give her the pills but you certainly didn't care afterward. You were pissed, but as you started to see her blossom with your kid, you wanted her to be pregnant. You want to own her, to possess her, to keep her as your own. You love that Bishop couldn't touch her heart.

Deep down, you're as big a monster as Reaper, only he got there first.

No matter what you do, she will always be bound to Reaper.

After the third man died, the fighting was over.

Dog came into the ring and he signaled the end and for people to pay up.

Preacher wasn't ready to stop fighting but he knew he had to hold back now. His need to spill blood was so strong. He waited as people paid their dues and left the building. One look at Dog, and he wanted to hurt him.

"I'm guessing no one has ever been stupid enough to take you on," Dog said.

"I suggest you get ready."

Dog smiled. "What makes you think I ever need to get ready for a blood bath? I'm always prepared."

He started out by sparring with Dog. The other man was fast and surprisingly agile. He didn't know why he was shocked. There was no extra information on who Dog was. Just the rumors of what he'd been born into believing. He wasn't a real person, he was a monster, and other such shit. Thinking about it now, Dog had a bad life.

Hitting him only created a little bit of pleasure. There was no lasting relief. Being hit back, there was the kicker he wanted. The adrenaline. The pain. The need to feel something because if he didn't, he was going home, fucking Robin until she was knocked up with his kid, and killing Bishop and Reaper. It was the least he could do after everything they'd put him through.

Robin pregnant.

Robin with Reaper's baby.

Robin having feelings for Reaper.

It was fucking wrong.

A MONSTER'S BEAUTY

All of a sudden, he was locked down on the ground. Dog was over him, keeping him in place.

"Get the fuck off me."

"Not until you calm the fuck down. I mean it, Preach. Calm the fuck down. Everyone has gone home and I don't want to kill you. You're not dead and I get it, you fight like a fucking beast, a monster. You're an animal and I recognize it." Dog still didn't let him go. "This isn't worth dying over."

He gritted his teeth, angry, enraged to know it didn't matter.

You're better than this.

Slowly, the darkness swarming in front of his vision eased and Dog slowly took his time to let go. "I don't need you hugging the shit out of me."

"You can be pissed all you want. You didn't feel how fucked up that was. The crowd went crazy. I don't know how we're going to top that shit."

Dog burst out laughing. "The cleaning crew is going to have a field day."

Preacher left the ring and went to the changing room where his jacket was, left untouched. He pulled it on, not caring as his body started to ache and hurt just like the good old days. This was one of the reasons he had to stop fighting. He had a club that needed him and he had to admit to getting too old.

"Do you want to talk about it?"

"I don't want to talk about shit," he said. All he really wanted was to forget.

"No, you want to kill stuff, which is fine with me. What I don't want is your ass in jail."

"I won't be. I'm more careful than that. Why do you think I came here?" He grabbed his keys and was about to leave.

"I can kill him for you," Dog said. "Strictly off

the table. No change of money. No hands dealt. I can kill him, make it look like a drive-by or some shit. A guy like that has a lot of enemies. All it would take is the click of my fingers and he'd be dead. You could look at your girl without worry, without guilt. It would all be on me, no one else."

Preacher looked back at his friend and nodded his head. "But I'd still know, and I'd have to be the one to look her in the eyes when she asks me what happened. I don't want to lie to her. She's been through enough already."

"You know, this girl, she's supposed to love you and only you, yet all I can see is a lot of fucking heartache. Do you want to tell me about that shit?"

"There's nothing to tell." He and Dog may be friends, but it didn't mean they were close. He never made that kind of mistake.

After leaving the warehouse, he straddled his bike, and without looking back, he took off into the night, riding his bike. With each passing hour, his body started to hurt and ache. He recognized the signs and it was a fucking bitch of all pain.

Finally, seeing no other reason not to return home, he did so, letting himself in through the kitchen. It was there where he found Robin in a robe, her hair messed up, sipping some hot chocolate.

The moment she saw him, she was on her feet. "What happened?" She reached for his face as if to touch him, and he took her hands, kissing the tips of her fingers.

"It's nothing."

"Your face doesn't look like nothing. What happened?" she asked, concern edged in her voice.

"I had to do what I had to do." He didn't let go of her hand. He stared into her eyes, wanting something, anything. The pain in his body only seemed to be getting worse. "I need to take a bath."

He had to have some distance. Somewhere in this house was the bane of all of his problems, and Bishop was also out there. He had a couple of men on the case, and if Bishop even thought to leave town, the little prick was dead.

Bishop had stopped being a son to him some time ago, and he wasn't ashamed to admit he had no feelings when it came to the kid. All he wanted to do was hurt him. To make him pay for what he did. Right now, he wasn't in his right mind when it came to making decisions. Everything had been handed to him, and slowly, swiftly, it was all being taken away. Robin coming back into his life, her memories returning, then of course Reaper, and all the revelations afterward.

He entered his bedroom, removed his leather cut, took off his clothes, and threw them in a pile. He'd burn them as soon as he was washed.

Running himself a bath, he climbed into the tub and soaked his aching muscles. He heard the door open and knew she'd come to see him.

Opening his eyes, he saw she was she perched on the edge of the tub.

"You shouldn't be in here."

"You left so quickly. I wanted to make sure you're okay."

"I'm fine."

"Do you hate me?" she asked.

"No, I couldn't hate you."

"My dad does. He thinks I'm a whore."

Preacher's hands clenched into fists. There was a lot of shit going on and he couldn't keep pandering to her needs, not anymore. "You're not a whore. He doesn't think that."

"He does and told me himself. But you're angry with me. I don't know what's worse."

"Yes, I'm angry. Not with you specifically. With the entire fucked-up circumstances. Surely you of all people understand it."

"I do. I know I haven't been the best person here, but I am trying, I promise." Tears filled her eyes, and he knew she was struggling with everything.

He lifted up in the water, taking her hand and locking their fingers together. "I'm with you. I don't hate you. I could never hate you. I'm angry you even had to make that choice."

She started to sob and he pulled her into his arms, not caring that he soaked through her pajamas. He had to hold her.

"There's something you don't know," she said, sniffling. "I ... I'm his wife."

"What?"

"Bishop signed the annulment papers. I was married before I even gave birth to Bethany. Please, don't be mad."

Preacher let her go. "I need you to leave."

"Preacher?"

"Get out," he said.

She didn't argue with him and he watched her go. Climbing out of the bathtub, he didn't care about his nakedness. He walked downstairs, and there was Reaper. The cause of all of his problems.

"Oh, sorry, did I wake you?" he asked as he grabbed the man's jacket and pulled him out of his slumber, throwing him across the room. His naked dick swung in the wind as he threw Reaper out of his house, heading into the back garden.

Preacher hadn't even bothered with some slippers to protect his feet. He grabbed Reaper and slammed his fist against the man's throat, shocking him to the ground as he attacked him. Reaper choked. Preacher slammed his fists and kept on punching, wanting to hurt him. He did have the element of surprise, but it didn't last long before Reaper was on his feet and retaliating.

"I'm guessing you've found out all the fun and exciting details I wanted to keep private," Reaper said. "You know, like how I married your woman. That must sting a lot. All of this must hurt, big time."

He slammed his fist into the man's face again and again. There was no way he was going to allow Reaper to just mock or laugh, or be happy about this, about any of this.

Reaper only laughed. "It must kill you to share the love of a woman. The first woman you ever loved and she can't even give you the whole deal, can she? She shares her heart with me."

Wrapping his fingers around Reaper's neck, he pressed him down, bending him over the wall. It would be so easy to kill him.

"You did all of this on purpose, didn't you? All along when you were working with O'Klaren, you saw an opportunity and you took it."

Reaper choked.

Preacher had no choice but to loosen his hold, and Reaper gasped. "Of course, I did. I had nothing to do with her losing that baby, though. I had my own agenda from the start."

"So all of this is just so you can, what? Have a little fun? You wanted to hurt the girl who dared to fall in love with me?"

Reaper laughed. "You don't get it, even now. I happen to be in love with her. This isn't about you. At least, it's not about you anymore. No, this is about what I feel, and I want her all to myself. I should promote your son. He gave me everything I ever wanted, I just didn't even realize it."

Preacher squeezed his throat.

"Kill me," Reaper said, choking out the words.

He wanted to.

You're better than this.

Win her back.

Slowly, he let go of the bastard's throat and stepped back.

"It's not over." With that, he entered the house to find Bear standing in the kitchen. The sound of Bethany crying came downstairs, and Preacher knew he was the problem.

"You should have killed him."

"Last time I checked, I don't take orders from you." He walked past Bear. "And the next time you call Robin a whore, you and I will have a whole big issue and you won't like it."

****

The following morning, Robin arrived at the library. She'd walked there from Preacher's house as she needed the space. After feeding Bethany, she'd placed her in the stroller Reaper had brought with him, leaving a note for the men to find when they woke up.

She couldn't be there to confront them, not after last night. She had to get away, to have some space.

You're being selfish.

No matter how selfish it was, she had to do it in order to be free.

Seeing the pain in Preacher's eyes last night, the way he'd ordered her away, it hurt more than anything she'd ever experienced in her life. This was a nightmare. How could she walk away from Preacher when just not being with him hurt more than anything else in her life? Yet, Reaper, why was she even struggling with this decision? It was all fucking wrong. It was nothing but a pain in her ass, every single second of it.

It was late when she finally got to the library, and she let herself through the doors to find Anne already behind the counter, serving a couple of kids.

"Hello … oh my, are you okay?"

"I'm fine. I'd like you to meet Bethany, my daughter."

"Last time I checked, you didn't have a kid, Robin."

"Yeah, well, a lot has since happened in my life, and believe me, none of it has been easy. It's quiet. How do you feel about some coffee and a chat?"

"Why not?"

Robin went to put the kettle on while Anne entertained Bethany. After taking her out of the stroller, they placed her in the kids' section, which was empty. Anne had to keep going back and serving customers but there were so few of them, Robin was able to get through the sorry tale of her love life and current issues without too many interruptions. Just saying them out loud was enough to make her ill. She didn't want drama or complications. What happened to being the sane one of the club, where she helped? Since the moment Milly had done what she did, that bitch had set an entire path of pain. One Robin didn't want to deal with but seemed to constantly be immersed in.

"Well, what do you think?"

"Wow, I'm kind of wow. That's a lot to process."

She left out the vital parts of murder and death, but other than that, she pretty much kept to the story. Of course, she didn't need to know she was given the date rape drug the first time around, so Anne didn't have all the facts.

"Yeah."

"And this guy, Bethany's father, he's here now?"

"Yep. A nice added complication."

"How do you feel about that? I mean really feel."

"I don't know. I honestly don't know what to do. I don't ... do you think I should move out? Or find another place to live? I need to be on my own. I don't know if I can be on my own. Everything is so fucked up."

"I ... I mean, it's an option as are all of these things. This kind of makes my issues with my husband seem pointless. I don't have two men vying for my affection."

"I don't have two men. They just want to kill each other. In all honesty, I don't even know if they love me. I mean, I know Preacher does. I hope he does, he has every right to hate me though. I've done nothing but cause him pain, heartache. Reaper, I don't know what to think about him. He took me to hurt Preacher, I'm sure of that. I don't know if he loves me, or loves the idea of hurting him."

"I, no, it doesn't matter," Anne said.

"Please, talk to me. I'm surrounded by a lot of hatred right now. My best friend, well, he's one of the reasons I'm here in this predicament."

"Yeah, I'd want to beat the crap out of Bishop for what he did but you can't take back any of this. You were happy with Preacher?"

"Yes, really happy."

"And with Reaper?"

"Not in the beginning. I was taken and then I guess I made the best of the situation, you know? Trying to find that silver lining. Wow, can you even hear me right now? I made the best of a bad situation? How horrible do I sound?" She nibbled on her lip. "I'm an asshole."

Anne laughed. "You're not an asshole and I'm not stupid either. I guess you've left a lot of details out. But how do you feel about Reaper now?"

"Guilty, angry, sad. I'm confused because I've been with Preacher now, and I guess I'd resigned myself to a life with Reaper and I'd tried to forget what it's like to be with him, you know?"

"I don't know why you should feel guilty. I mean, yes, you've got some issues as we all do, but at the end of the day, you were hurt, badly. You've made some bad decisions along the way, but you can't be held responsible for all of them, can you?"

"I have to." She ran fingers through her hair then finished off her coffee. "I made this choice. I could have … ignored these feelings."

"Robin, you were young and on your own in a bad situation. Have you ever considered you need therapy? The guy kidnapped you, and I'm guessing it wasn't always good."

Robin tried not to think of the early days of being with Reaper. It wasn't good. In fact, it was painful. The very thought of it filled her with dread. "A lot happened, I can tell you that."

"We've been looking everywhere for you," Bear said.

She looked up as her father came into the library, letting his presence be known.

"Dad," she said.

"Reaper and Preacher are looking for you. You shouldn't go out on your own. You know it's not fucking safe."

"Language," Anne said. "You're in a library where children come and there's a little girl right there."

Bear sneered. "It's the spawn of fucking Satan, is what it is, and this is none of your business."

"My business or not, get out of my library, or I swear, I will call Billy and I don't care what kind of friendship you have. I will have you locked up so fast you won't know what to do with yourself. You have no right to come in here and spewing your hatred. She's a little girl and doesn't deserve your spite. You call yourself a man? You're worthless." Anne stepped up to him. "Now, get out."

Bear glared at the woman and Robin saw a little admiration in his gaze.

"Do you want me to give you a countdown? Your cut doesn't scare me."

"I'll be outside, Robin. Don't make the wrong decision here. It will end badly for you."

She watched her father go and felt even more deflated. "Great," she said.

Getting to her feet, she picked Bethany up, who started to fuss because she didn't want to leave.

"So, that's your father."

"Yep. It's him. I better be going."

"Robin, I'm always here if you need me. All you've got to do is ask for help."

"I don't need help right now, Anne. I need a miracle. I'm hoping to still come to work, but knowing my luck, I'll probably be banned from coming or something." She shrugged.

"Just so you know, I think you have the answer to your problem, you're just afraid of making the wrong choice. This isn't about how those men think or feel. You've got to think about what it is you want. Otherwise, you're going to spend the rest of your life making the best of it. Just remember, one of them had you smiling, the other, you were making the best of a bad decision."

She placed her daughter into the stroller, secured her in place, and moved away, saying thank you to Anne.

A MONSTER'S BEAUTY

Once she left the library, she found her dad smoking a cigarette outside.

"She's a lively woman," he said.

"I know. That's Anne for you."

"She's married."

"I guess you haven't heard the gossip then."

"What gossip?"

"Her husband sleeps around. She knows about it and puts up with it because of the kids." She shrugged. "She deserves better but she will do whatever she has to for her children."

"I know."

"How would you know? You slept around on Mom."

"I know, but she deserved it. She was fucking everything in sight. We were both as bad as each other."

"You really hate me, don't you?" she asked. Again, she felt close to tears and it was all becoming a little too much for her.

Bear stared at her. "No, I don't hate you."

"You think I'm a whore."

"Again, I didn't mean to … I … I'm angry, okay? You don't know what it's been like to be with Preacher while he was hunting for you, and to find this." He pointed at her and then Bethany.

She nodded her head, pressing her lips together. "Of course. I mean, it wouldn't be like I'd have a choice, would it?"

"Robin!"

"No, you don't know what happened and you don't understand anything. You're judging me and you know what? It's fine. You can judge me. I don't care." She pushed her daughter away. "It's okay, sweetheart. I know it's going to be tough, but we've got to make a decision and I believe I've already found it. I've just got to be brave enough to do this."

    She didn't look back at her dad. Instead, she kept on moving forward, knowing in her heart the only way she'd be able to deal with her life right now was to take a step back from the club, from Preacher, from everything. It was the only way she was going to survive this.

Chapter Three

"What the fuck is this?" Preacher asked.

"It's an apartment near the library. The rent is good and I know I can make a living for me and Bethany," Robin said.

Bear cursed and got up. "This is fucking ridiculous."

Preacher had been taking care of business and looking for Robin when he'd gotten the call that she wanted to talk to him. Reaper, of course, was present. The bastard was everywhere he turned. He went from not being able to locate him, to not being able to take a piss without the prick being there with his smiling face. It was like he was mocking him with his presence, and he hated it. Still, at least with him close by, he didn't have to worry about if the guy was going to be attacking him anytime soon.

Robin ignored Bear and looked at him.

"Let me get this straight, you want to leave my house?"

"I think it's best. For me, for Bethany, for the clubs. I know this can't be easy on anyone and I know some of the men are already pissed at me."

"Robin, be careful," Bear said.

"I don't have to listen to you." She turned to Bear. "I've thought about this. Your feelings toward me, to the whole situation. You think you're the only one who feels this way? No, I don't. I believe there will be other people who feel the same, and staying here isn't safe for me."

"Robin, this is the safest place for you," Reaper said.

"No, it's not. I want... I've done everything everyone has asked of me, my entire life. I followed

Bishop around, and I did what you asked for when I got pregnant," she said.

"I only wanted to protect you," Preacher said.

"I know. So, I married Bishop. Then I lost the baby and we ... it went on, and then I was taken, and this happened, and I need space. You both want me to pick you and to make the right decision in all of this and I can't. I've only just got my memories back and you want me to be your wife," she said, pointing at Reaper. "I don't know who she is anymore because I came home and I know what it's like to be with Preacher. I can't do this anymore. I won't." She sat back and took a breath.

Preacher saw the determination in her face.

"This is my decision. I'm not asking for permission to do what I need to do. I'm telling you I'm moving into this apartment, and I'm not getting in the way of club business. Whatever you guys need to sort out, deal with it, because I'm not getting in the middle. I won't. I'm done. I feel like I've already wasted enough of your guys' time, and it's now for me to leave and to find a place for myself."

"How do you expect to support you and Bethany?" Preacher asked.

"Working hard. I can budget, I always have. I can do this. I know I can."

Bear laughed. "You're not cut out for the big wide world, Robin. This is all a fallacy."

"I'm not cut out for the big wide world, huh? I guess being raped and beaten, used as a bargaining tool, hurt, humiliated, and forced to marry a guy I didn't want... I mean, what else is there? I've lost my memories, gained them back, lost a kid, got a kid. Yeah, I'm not ready for the big wide world. What can I not do?" she asked. "At the end of the day, if I struggle to make ends meet, I could always, I don't know, become the whore you think I am."

"Enough!" Preacher heard the pain in her voice, the anger, the regret. He looked at Bear, who had also gone silent. "We need to stay calm."

"No other man will touch you," Reaper said. "If you call her a whore again, I will cut your dick off, shove it in your mouth, and make you eat it before getting a bat and fucking you in the ass, and getting my boys to use you one by one. Do you understand?"

Preacher slammed his hand against the table. "You're not a whore. This is… It's not safe for you. You don't have to do this."

"You think I didn't see what you did last night after I told you the truth that I'm married to him? I can't look at your face, Preacher. I'm not stupid and I'm not blind. I'm the cause of all of this and I can end all of this by not giving in. By not being this way. A fresh start with my daughter. You and Reaper can resolve your issues. No more pain. No more anything."

"You're our issue," Reaper said.

Robin pressed her lips together and stared down at her lap, hands clenched tightly together. She sniffled. "I know and you all want me to make some kind of choice, and I can't do that. I'm sorry. I'm confused. I…" She looked at Bear.

"Leave," Preacher said.

"She's my daughter. I can stay here. Whatever she has to say, I have a right to know."

"And I'm your president. You want to take me on, bring it on. This is personal and private. You no longer get the chance to be here when you put all the blame on her and called her a whore."

Bear laughed. "Am I the only one seeing the problem is her? This isn't a hard choice to make. You take Preacher. You take what you want and you don't allow her to cloud your fucking mind."

"Get out," Preacher said and this time Reaper stood.

"You think you can take me on?" Bear asked.

Without another word, Robin got to her feet. "And this is why I have to leave. Bear has every right to be here, not me. I'm the problem and I'm tired of being in the middle. I know this should be an easy decision, but it's not. As much as I hate to admit it, I love you both. I can't pick and I won't. Bethany needs a father and I … I can't. I, I'm leaving. She will just have to cope with having a mother."

She left the table and he heard her pick up the phone.

Looking at Bear and then Reaper, he didn't like what was happening, but he knew she was making the right decision for her. He had to deal with each little problem element. First, this situation with Reaper and his club, Bear, his own club, and then his feelings for Robin.

She didn't come back into the room and he heard her move upstairs.

"You're just going to let her go?" Reaper asked.

"There's no letting going on right now," Preacher said.

"It's not safe for her."

"You should have thought about that before you brought your child here to deal with all of this." Preacher left the room. "Try not to kill each other," he said as a parting shot.

After walking upstairs, he went to her bedroom where she had a single case open with some clothes put inside.

She turned toward him and he saw the tears in her eyes. "I'm sorry. I'm really sorry."

He couldn't have her crying. He went straight to

her and pulled her into his arms, kissing the top of her head and knowing he'd never let her go. His love for her was absolute. "I know you need to go and I even understand the reason. But I don't want you to go. Last night, I fucked up, I wasn't ready for that little fact."

She sniffled. "I never wanted this to happen. Any of this. For so long, I waited for you, hoping you'd find me. I begged and prayed you would."

He closed his eyes, breathing her in. "I failed."

"No, I failed. I stopped fighting. I no longer believed and I gave in, and in doing so, I gave you up. I should choose Reaper. I've already caused you so much pain."

"Don't."

"But." She licked her lips. "You gave yourself to me. You shared details of your life with me, and I can't stop caring about you. I can't walk away from the way you make me feel. I don't want to."

He reached out to stroke her cheek. "You don't have to. I'm not giving up on you."

"You can't stand to look at Bethany."

"I don't know her. This is a lot to take in. Give me time." He pulled her close, kissing her head. "I love you, Robin."

She started to sob against him. "I love you too. I'm so sorry but I've got to put Bethany first in all of this. She doesn't deserve any of this."

"Don't be sorry. If you ever need anything, you'll come to me." He thought about Dog. "You also need to come to dinner Sunday."

She sniffled as she pulled back. Her eyes swollen and bloodshot. "Why?"

"I've got a deal with a guy. He helped me when I needed it most and as part of his agreement to help me, he wanted to have a dinner with you there."

"Oh."

"Yeah, so, I guess I was wondering how you'd feel about that?" he asked.

"You really need me there?"

"Yes. It was his suggestion."

"I can do that for you." She went on her toes, kissing his cheek. "I love you, Preacher. I'll be here Sunday."

There was a knock on the door.

"Who did you call?"

"Anne. She said if I ever needed her, I could give her a call. I guess it wasn't an empty promise." She sniffled. "Thank you, Preacher, for understanding. My dad, he … he's having a hard time dealing."

"I know. I'll talk to him." He watched her finish with her case as someone let Anne in downstairs.

Preacher wanted to fight, to tell her to stay, but he also saw the necessity of her being on her own. Keeping her away would mean he could take care of business and win her back. This was a competition with Reaper, and he had no doubt his opponent was already figuring out ways to get to her first and win her heart. All Preacher knew was there was something he was missing, and he needed to find it. Once he did, he'd have Robin back.

****

"Thank you for doing this," Robin said.

"Don't worry about it. It's nice to have someone else at home," Anne said. "The kids will be out tomorrow, but my husband is home."

"Will he mind me staying with you?" Robin asked, looking into the back to see Bethany already passed out. Her daughter could sleep through anything, it would seem. Even her own mother feeling like she was tearing apart from the inside out.

"It doesn't matter if he does or not. He's going to

have to get used to it because it's my life too and well, I've had to put up with many things from him." Anne's grip on the steering wheel tightened. "I have to say I'm a little envious."

"Of me?"

"Yes."

Robin chuckled. "Okay, I need to know how you could possibly be envious of me after all I've told you."

"Those two men. Yeah, they're bikers and I know you're going through a lot right now, but come on, Robin. Look at them and tell me they're not hunks. I mean, you're twenty-one and I guess there's a draw there."

"It's not my age. I hope it's not my age. I'll be getting older soon."

"I saw the way both men looked at you. Believe me, it's more than your age. They are both completely in love with you. It must be nice."

"Don't you have anyone admiring you?"

"Nope. Not me." She shrugged. "I've been a married woman for so long I probably don't even know what flirting is. Most men look at me like I'm a nag or something."

"You're not a nag. Do you and your husband go out?"

"Nope. Elijah likes to go out with other people. I guess it's working for us. I don't know. Also, I do nag."

Robin didn't for a second believe it was working for her friend. If anything, it sounded like Anne was incredibly lonely, and she'd been working at the library for a few months now, only to discover her friend was … hurting. She felt sad and a little selfish. Not once did she really take the time to think about what Anne was going through. "I'm sorry."

"Don't be. Although, he may hit on you. I'm not

sure though. He's never done it when I'm around, but if he does ... unless you want to, that is—"

"Anne, I'm not going to try to date your husband or hook up with him. I've got my own problems and besides, you're the closest person I've got to a friend right now. There's no way I'd betray your trust like that, believe me."

"You'd be surprised how many women want him, and even some of them claimed to be my friends as well. They would smile to my face and screw my husband behind my back."

"They're not your friends. You've had shitty friends. I'll show you what a good friend is like. It's fine. I won't even look at your husband. I promise." Her friendship with Anne was far more important than any man. She didn't want to meet Elijah. He sounded like one of the worst kinds of men to be attached to.

Arriving at Anne's house, she was taken aback by how big it was.

"Yeah, I think my husband's draw is that he makes a lot of money," Anne said.

"Your house is beautiful."

"You've yet to see the inside."

"Are we bragging now?" she asked.

"Little bit. Come on. At least I have something to brag about and you'll have a nice place to stay at with me."

Robin grabbed Bethany from the car. This was only a temporary accommodation until she was able to move into an apartment. She'd already gotten the details on a place and put herself on the waiting list.

The moment they entered Anne's house, noise and chaos started. It wasn't bad either. It brought a smile to her lips. She felt it was a nice change after the quiet stillness of Preacher's place. Silence didn't offer her any kind of comfort.

A young boy, he couldn't have been older than ten, charged toward his mother, holding her. "Emma's being mean again."

"Of course she is."

"She's saying when she goes to college I'm going to be forgotten."

"Ignore your sister." Anne ran her fingers through her son's hair. "There's no way you can be forgotten. Your farts stink too bad."

"I should fart in a jar for her. Let her take it with her all the way to college."

"Robin, I'd like you to meet my son, Elijah Junior. Junior, this is my friend Robin."

Elijah Junior pulled away from his mother. His face went beet red as he mumbled something to her. He left only for two of Anne's daughters to come down to greet them.

Robin didn't recognize either of them, and then there was Elijah, Anne's husband.

"What took you so long?" Elijah asked. "I expected you back an hour ago, and who is this?"

One look at him, and she didn't like him. Maybe it was knowing he'd cheated on Anne and made her put up with it or what, but Robin couldn't stand him. Then of course there was the way he spoke to her, as if Anne had purposefully annoyed him.

"This is Robin Keats. She works with me. How about I get you settled?"

"Sounds great."

"Wait, Keats? You're Bishop's wife?"

Robin looked at him. She didn't say a word. She didn't owe this man any other kind of explanation.

"Is she deaf?"

"No, I'm not deaf, I don't have to say who I'm

married to or not." It was also kind of embarrassing. Reaper had never once told her his real name. How ... strange was that? She didn't know his real first or last name, so her marriage certificate had been granted to Reaper. She had no way of knowing.

"Anne, I think we need to talk about this," Elijah said.

"What? This is my house as well and I can invite whomever I want to stay over. Robin needs a place to stay, and well, she's a friend. Besides, I thought you had a PA to go screw, or should I keep my voice down so the kids don't know?" Anne asked.

"You're ... we need to talk about this."

"There's nothing to talk about. You get to do what you want, and now I get to do what I want. It's fair. Come on."

Robin followed close behind Anne as they walked upstairs to one of the many rooms.

"Here you go. It was an office, but after everything happened, I threw out all of his office stuff, and now it's a spare bedroom for any occasion."

"Is this where you sleep?"

"No, no, I have my own room, but this should do, right? I pulled out the old crib for you. I've been meaning to throw it out. I'm not having any more kids, but I don't know, I couldn't seem to part with it." Anne stroked the crib. "It was a different time in my life."

"How are you coping now?"

"I'm coping. For the kids. I think it's easier on them if I'm home and acting the part of doting wife."

"They have no idea he cheats on you?"

"They don't need to know, you know. It's one of those ... things. The bed is comfortable. I've also picked up some milk and food for her. She looks big and strong. Can I hold her?"

A MONSTER'S BEAUTY

"Of course."

Robin held the car seat with two hands as Anne grabbed Bethany out of it. When it was empty, she placed it in the corner. Anne clearly didn't want to talk about her life with Elijah and she knew all about the pain of not wanting to know her past, so she left it.

"I'm going to go and get the bags. I'll be back."

She left Anne holding her daughter as she rushed out of the house, grabbing the two cases she'd been able to pack, and made her way inside.

After flicking the lock into place, she turned around to see Elijah standing there, watching her.

"You better not take any advantage of my wife."

Robin couldn't help it, she laughed. "You're talking to me about taking advantage. You need to look in the mirror to know what advantage looks like." This man was clearly crazy. He had to be to think she would take advantage when this guy was doing it every single day.

"She told you?"

"Yeah, and besides, if she didn't, there was already a whole load of gossip around town. You think this place doesn't know how to spread rumors? Nearly everyone knows what you do, and with who."

"I don't like you being near my wife."

"And I don't like men like you who take what they want and hurt whoever the hell they want to in the process, but we can't always have what we want, can we?"

"Your husband is a criminal."

"And you're a cheating scumbag who humiliates his woman all the time. You make a mockery of your marriage to Anne and you take all of this for granted." Robin took a deep breath. "Are you done with the judgment? Can I go? This can go any kind of way you want it to."

"When I find a way, you're gone."

Robin shrugged. "This isn't permanent. But if I can get her to leave your ass, then I'll consider it a job well done. She deserves a real man who will treat her with respect." In a way, just the few minutes with this man reminded her a little of Bishop.

There was a selfishness to him, something she didn't like in anyone, but witnessing it in Elijah made her even angrier. Maybe because it was directed toward someone she cared about rather than herself. With Bishop, in a way, she could accept it. He was a guy but he also didn't have any other responsibilities. This man, he had a wife, a family, and he was tearing it apart in order to have his fun.

No, she didn't like him.

Anne was a strong woman and she admired her for her ability to not let this man get to her. Others wouldn't have been quite so accommodating. Thinking about Preacher stepping out on her was enough to make her sick. The feelings for Reaper weren't the same. She'd experienced jealousy but nothing like this. With Reaper, it was like she expected it. He would grow bored with her and whatever his reasons were for taking her. No, she wouldn't think about this, not right now. All of her feelings were new to her, and not at any point were they exciting. For the most part, she was angry.

Moving around Elijah, she walked back up toward the bedroom where Anne was still holding Bethany.

"Hey, I'm sorry, I should have gotten Elijah to move them."

"No, worries. I've done it. And I think the less contact I have with your husband, the better."

"What's he done?"

"He's done nothing. Don't worry. I don't like him and it's not a crime to not like someone."

"So, I was thinking the kids are going to a friend's sleepover tomorrow night. How about we have some girl time? The library is closed this Monday, and I can get Elijah to drop the kids off at school."

"I'd love to." Robin winced. "I can't."

"Oh, it's fine."

"No, I've got a dinner I need to attend. Preacher needs me there, but how about you come to Sunday dinner? I can ask him and we can both go. It could be fun and if you're there, I know I can get home. There won't be any death or anything. We'd all be on our best behavior. Believe me, I don't know if I can handle the thought of dinner right now, and you'd be helping me out a lot."

"Your life sounds very exciting."

In Robin's mind, she instantly thought about losing her first child. "It's not, believe me, you wouldn't love my life at all."

"I don't know. Two men vying for your affection. A baby, and I bet they wouldn't cheat on you for a secretary or anything, would they?"

"I honestly don't know."

"It must be nice."

"It is nice."

Anne placed a sleeping Bethany into the crib, running fingers through her hair. "I know you're having a hard time with everything. I'm sorry if I'm seeming a little … callous."

"You're not. You're far from callous. Believe me, it's fine. I like that you treat me normal, like I won't break at a moment's notice. I'm not different to you, and I like that."

"Will you pick between the two?" Anne asked.

"Eventually, I mean."

Robin sat down on the bed with a heavy sigh. "I don't know. I don't know what I'm going to do." She blew out a breath. "A lot has happened in such a short space of time, you know? Old feelings, new feelings, they're all combining and I'm more confused now than I've ever been. It's a lot to take in. I know it's wrong but I sometimes wish I could go back to not remembering, you know? It would be a hell of a lot easier."

"It's not wrong. Your life wasn't as simple as you thought it would be. It makes a lot of sense for you to want to stop it, put your life on hold. If you ever need to talk about it, you know where to find me."

"Thank you for all of this. I really needed to have some space to call my own."

"Oh, to see the look on his face. I can't deny there was a huge thrill in defying him. You're welcome to stay for as long as you like." Anne patted her knee with a smile. "I better go and see what he's doing. I haven't heard him leave yet and I don't want his date coming here and starting something, not with the kids still home. If you're hungry, I'll make you a sandwich."

"I am. I'll be down in a moment."

"Yeah, please, and save me from him." Anne didn't look afraid.

"Anne, why do you put up with it?" Robin asked.

Anne held the door as she stopped. "I don't know."

"Did it ever hurt you to find out the truth?"

"The first couple of times, yeah. I don't know why I stayed, apart from the kids. I know a lot of families make it work. I didn't … it felt important to stay together but also, the longer we're together, the pain has become nonexistent. He can't hurt me anymore. I just expect him to follow rules, like keeping the kids in the dark for as long as possible. What I don't ever want them to think is I'm a fool."

"You're not a fool, Anne."

"I know, but a lot of people would see it that way. I better go. Don't keep me waiting long."

She left the door open as she left and Robin looked down at her daughter. "I hope I'm making the right decision here, for you, for me." She reached out and stroked her cheek. An overwhelming love rushed through her as she looked at her sleeping daughter. "I wish you came with all the answers, sweetheart. I could really use them right now." Nothing came from Bethany. Taking another big deep breath, she watched her sleep, finding peace in seeing her little girl.

Her stomach chose that moment to growl and so she grabbed the baby monitor on the drawer beside the bed and made her way downstairs.

"This is my house. I should have a say who's in it and who isn't."

"Really? Well, as my husband, your body should belong to me, and seeing as I can't have a say in that, then I don't see why you should get a say in this. Robin's staying. Is this because she hasn't giggled in your presence like a little schoolgirl? I know how you like them young, Elijah. Are you wanting to screw my new best friend? Is that it? You want to prove you can have any woman you want and you're not just an old married man who has lost everything?"

Robin entered the kitchen and what she saw made her feel cold. From where she stood, it looked like Elijah had his hands wrapped around her throat and was about to hit her, but Anne's smile didn't portray any kind of fear.

"Sandwich?"

Chapter Four

"This is a big old mistake," Bear said.

"From the moment Robin left, you've been telling me what a big old mistake this was. In fact, she didn't even have to leave for you to feel this was a giant mistake," Preacher said, testing his gravy. It needed a little more salt and pepper. He added in some more, not too much, because he knew how much Robin loved his gravy, and he wanted this meal to be perfect. At least, some parts of it. When the fuck did he care about his food? He wasn't about to share his thoughts with Bear or anyone else. This was a dinner for a deal, nothing more.

So far, Dog was on his way, alone as he didn't want or need any of his boys present. Bear was also here, as was Reaper. The leader of Slaves to the Beast hadn't left his home, and all night Preacher had been struck with an overwhelming desire to help the bastard meet his untimely end. First, he needed Robin to make any kind of decision. The last thing he wanted to do was hurt her. The temptation was strong though.

People had accidents all the time. Falling down the stairs, tripping, electrocution, Reaper could find himself on the end of being pushed or helped down the death traps. It would be so easy, especially as he could just reach out to Dog, who'd made it clear he'd take care of it. Instead, he'd dreamed about Robin. Watching her with a new family, seeing a darkness lurking over her, but being unable to stop whatever was about to happen because she couldn't see the truth, and he had to be the one to see her get hurt, to witness her die by the man she thought she could trust. Dreams weren't real. He had to protect Robin at all costs because even though dreams were meaningless, he still felt they held an edge of truth.

He didn't trust or believe Reaper, and there was

something he was missing. Some random piece of information that could be vital for him to win. He had no doubt with Bethany being Reaper's daughter, there was a chance Robin would try to do the right thing, but he wouldn't let her or her daughter get hurt. She shouldn't be making the right decision for her daughter; no, she should be making the choice for herself and her future happiness.

Reaper may be Bethany's father, but Preacher wouldn't let it interfere with his need to protect, nor would he hold it against the little girl. She had no say in who her father was, and besides, it wasn't about whose cum it was that fathered her. It was all about the man she called father, and he would quite happily take the role. He'd come to that decision just last night, sleeping alone with no Robin in his home, in his arms. He'd do anything to keep her and if that meant being a dad to a child that wasn't his, he'd do it, for her, for himself.

He'd made a mistake when he'd told Robin to get out of the bathroom. Whatever had caused her to become Reaper's wife, he had to remember in the beginning, she was hoping and praying for him. His inability to get to her forced her to make the best of what she had. The truth was, she'd given up hope and he needed to remind her that when it came to Reaper, she'd given up, not made a choice.

The doorbell rang and Preacher left Bear alone with the food to answer the door. Hopefully not spoiling it in the process. Bishop was on the doorstep, carrying some beers.

"Bear called me and I guess I want to make amends for what I've done. I know you hate me, and I'm probably on the last couple of weeks if not months of my life, but I am sorry. To you, to Robin. I want … I want to make it up to you in any way I can."

"You can come in for dinner, but don't start shit. I'm not in the mood or interested."

"Ah, so the loving son returns again. I'm shocked you've accepted him back with open arms. I didn't think you had it in you," Reaper said. "You know, with him being a traitor to you. When it comes to what Bishop wants, everyone has to suffer."

"Did you set the table?" He wouldn't react. There was a time and place for this.

"What? You're not going to bite? Remember we're all in this mess because of Bishop."

"Actually, we're in this mess because you couldn't handle me being happy. This is all because you *forcibly* took what is mine. So keep bringing it up. If Robin keeps on hearing you, it'll remind her who you really are and what you do."

Silence met his response. He was done with this conversation.

"Have you set the table?" he asked again.

"This is all very domestic of you. Maybe I should marry you, Preacher, have you as my bitch, and yes, I set the table."

Preacher ignored the jibe and made his way into the kitchen, grabbing one of his cool beers from the fridge.

"You do realize how messed up this all is and sounds, right?"

"What?"

"Dinner with Dog because he helped you out," Bear said.

"I have to pay my debts off somehow and seeing as the club is already pissed at me, I figured offering to sell off the girls wouldn't exactly work."

"No, it wouldn't," Bear said. "The boys are all a little tense with Reaper being in town and his club not too far behind him. They're all waiting for a war and of course, they're nervous about what you did to Grave."

Preacher finished mashing his potatoes and then draining his sprouts. It was a little early for a Christmas dinner, but with the last-minute notice of cooking, he settled on ease. The door went again. He left Bear with the sprouts as he went to answer the door. He was surprised to see Dog in a suit.

He couldn't recall ever seeing the man in anything other than a wifebeater shirt and jeans. This was all new. Oddly strange for him to put in any kind of effort.

"You do know I'm cooking, right? I'm not some fancy chef."

"Yeah, well, I'm entering a war zone and I've come armed. I didn't know if you'd need some backup. Besides, it's respectful to show up at another's house looking all nice. It was one of the few things my parents taught me." Dog opened his jacket to display all the knives he had ready if the moment needed it. "All you've got to do is give me the all-clear, and I'll take out your problems right now. Even in front of your girl if that's necessary."

"I appreciate it. No bloodshed today."

Preacher wasn't about to complain about Dog being ready to start an all-out war. There were a couple of people in attendance he wanted to kill and if he blamed Dog, it wasn't his fault, but temptation aside, it wasn't going to happen today.

Just as he was about to close the door, another car pulled into the lot. It wasn't one he recognized, but the moment Robin climbed out, he didn't need to. She wore a black dress that stopped at the knee and molded to her curves. Anne, the woman she was currently staying with, was next to her.

The moment he realized she was staying with Anne, he intended to make sure his tech man and Billy ran a quick background check on the woman. Her only crime was marrying a man who was a complete and total asshole, and he couldn't hold that against her. There were a lot of assholes in the world, and many of them hid behind a suit.

"I hope it's okay that I invited Anne to come and have dinner with us."

"No problem at all. It seems I have a full house today. Where's Bethany?" he asked. He'd hoped the child would help him stay on the straight and narrow and not take Dog's opportunity to kill Reaper, and possibly Bishop.

"Anne knows a good babysitter who's taking care of Bethany. I didn't know if you'd want her here."

"I wouldn't have minded, but it's nice to see you. You're looking amazing, as always."

"You know how much I love flattery," she said, smiling.

Preacher took her hands and pulled her in close, kissing her cheek.

Reaper cleared his throat from behind him. Just another irritation to add to the mix.

"Preacher, I don't think I've ever introduced you to Anne. Anne, this is Preacher. He's the club president of Twisted Monsters MC."

"I know of you," Anne said. "Pleasure. It was about time we met."

"And this is Reaper. He's Bethany's father." Robin hadn't let go of his hand and Preacher wasn't about to do so unless she wanted it. Not having her in his bed was sheer torture, especially now, knowing there was a chance she may never be in his bed again. He was already working to find all of Reaper's dark secrets. With him staying close, it made hunting for all the information he needed a little easier. There had to be a reason Robin was taken, and he felt Reaper was the cause in some way. He had to hope he could win this fight, no matter how many dirty secrets he had to give up in the process.

"I know you," Anne said. "You came to the library. That's why I recognize Bethany. It's not because she looks like you at all, Robin."

"You went to the library?" Robin asked.

"I knew it was where you worked and I wanted to see you. I was giving up hope of ever having you in my life again."

"So you've been close the entire time I've been here?"

"I didn't want to lose you. I love you, and nothing will change that."

"I need to go and check on dinner," Preacher said. All these confessions were not sitting well with him. He needed a break.

"I'll come with you," Robin said.

They walked hand-in-hand toward the kitchen. Bear sat at the counter, dipping a fork into the mashed potatoes and eating.

"There better be enough for everyone," Preacher said.

Robin let go of his hand and he saw her looking at Bear. "I better go and make sure the guests aren't killing each other." Bear left the kitchen without another word to his daughter. Preacher gripped his kitchen tongs to flip the meat in the oven.

"I'm sorry about him," he said.

"It's fine. I figured it would take a little while for him to come around. I guess I was hoping for too much. You should probably be reacting the same way as him, after everything."

"It's not too much. With Reaper and now Dog here, tensions are at a new high. We're all worried about you and I'm not angry with you, or upset. You have nothing to worry about here."

"No need to be worried. Most of the time I can take care of myself. At least I like to tell myself that. I'm proving to be a bit of a liar in that department."

He smiled. "You're doing fine."

"Am I? I don't feel like I am." She sighed. "Sorry, I don't mean to put a downer on anything. I promise." She took a deep breath. "Is there anything you need help with?"

"You, sweetheart, can't cook." He wrapped his arms around her waist, holding her close. "I can do everything. I figured you wanted out of there for a reason," he said.

"Yeah, it's not easy with Reaper. He always seems to want the same, like he's trying to show everyone he's just as important as you. I don't know. Maybe he is."

"You know I've got a couple of questions about him and you. Do you think we could meet up sometime next week, talk about it?"

"I'd love to."

He nodded and let her go. He wanted to do more than let her go. Bending her over the counter, fucking her, and filling her tight cunt with his cum was what he wanted to do. Instead, he went back to finishing serving. He tried his gravy again, satisfied with the taste, and began to serve up into bowls.

Robin helped him carry everything. Once all of the food was at the table, he called for dinner. Robin took the seat next to his, and when Dog arrived, he sat opposite him at the other end of the table.

"Dog, I'd like you to meet Robin. Robin, this is

my good friend Dog."

After all the introductions were over with, people began to serve themselves. He carved the meat and passed it to those who wanted some meat and waited until people were ready and finished before sitting down and serving himself. Robin had already started to serve him.

One look at Reaper and he saw the other man was pissed, but he didn't give a fuck. Robin had served him for a long time. She'd lived in this house, been best friends with his son. They had a connection Reaper couldn't just wipe out no matter how hard he tried.

"This is rather nice. I've got to say I'm a little shocked to see this brat at your table, Preacher," Dog said, pointing at Bishop.

"I'm his son."

"And still a rat. I mean, come on, you handed his worst enemy the woman he loved out of petty teenage jealousy. That's got to be hard for you. With all due respect, I'd be using your head as an ornament."

"Er, Anne isn't part of any of the lifestyle," Robin said. "She's an … innocent?"

"Don't mind me, Robin. I find this fascinating." Anne sat opposite Bear and was beside Robin. Bishop was on her other side.

Eating had come to a stop.

"See, women like a bit of gossip and besides, sweetheart, there's a lot to be had at this table." Dog smiled at her.

"Oh, don't mind me. It's nice not to be the center of gossip," Anne said.

"You got a tale to tell?" Dog asked. "I'm all for hearing recent news."

"I don't think she wants to tell her personal business to you," Bear said.

"It's fine. My husband is a whore. He doesn't get paid for it, but he sleeps around with anything that will have him." Anne laughed. "He doesn't like Robin, though. Probably because she shut him down firmly last night."

"I have no interest in your husband."

"And he does like them young," Anne said.

"You're not sad about that?" Bishop asked.

"I have to do what I need to do for my kids. Staying with a man I can't stand, it's par for the course. Haven't you had to do something you can't stand?" Anne asked, looking at Bishop.

This time, Robin burst out laughing.

Preacher detected the signs of hysteria. He didn't stop Robin though. She needed to get this off her chest. "Believe me, Anne, he thinks he's God's gift to women, and yes, Bishop had to do a lot of stuff he didn't like. He had to take me to the doctor's to get my ultrasound, right? He didn't stick around or anything. It was too painful for him to deal with."

"You were carrying my brother or sister."

"Sister," Robin said. "And let me guess, it was all my fault again, huh? Yeah, Robin, the whore, she sleeps around with everyone. Getting knocked up was totally my idea. It had nothing to do with the jealousy of another woman because of you, right? No, that couldn't be it because in the scheme of things, you're completely blameless."

"Fascinating," Anne said.

"You could have gotten rid of it," Bishop said.

"I didn't want to. You wanted me to get rid of it and let me guess, what little Bishop wants, he gets. You're always like this. Always have been. A spoiled little brat, and you couldn't even handle being known as Preacher's son. What was it you used to call yourself,

A MONSTER'S BEAUTY

PMS!"

Bishop got to his feet.
Robin did as well and Preacher followed suit.
"Enough!"
Dog looked entertained.
This wasn't how he wanted his dinner to go. Fuck!

"What are you going to do, Bishop? You know I'm right and now you're back here, begging for forgiveness when the truth is this is your fault. Like a damn baby, you can't accept responsibility for your own actions."

"No, it's not. If you'd spread your legs for me, this wouldn't have been a problem. Milly was all about doing that."

"Yeah, the very woman who decided to drug me and got me knocked up in the process. Let's not forget about that. And there, my friends, is the truth. I refused to sleep with you, ended up knocked up by your dad, and it bugs you, doesn't it? Why don't you go run off? Plot some other form of revenge. You're good with that and blaming other people for your own issues." Robin slammed back down in her chair.

Her hand shook as she reached out for some water.

"I had no idea your family could be so entertaining," Dog said.

"Why is he even here?" Bishop asked.

"I asked to be here. This is a debt being dealt with. It's big boy stuff, you wouldn't understand."

"You're here to have your fun," Preacher said.

"I wasn't the one who accepted the man who kidnapped his woman, or the son who allowed it to happen."

"Can we stop, please?" Robin said. "This is …

look, as you can clearly see, this isn't easy for any of us and you're going to cause a lot more trouble that's not needed."

"Which one do you love?" Dog asked.

She dropped her fork. "Is this guy for real?"

"I can see you have issues when it comes to the boy, and I get it. There's an air of being spoiled around him, but your thoughts and feelings for Reaper and Preacher. What are they?"

"It's none of your business."

"Enough, Dog."

"Hear me out. I know I'm hitting on touchy fucking subjects and forgive me for not being tactful, but you got her pregnant first through an act of one of your club whores. Then, through the act of your son, she was taken from you, by this man. Now, I heard through the gossip how she was found. Beaten, broken, bruised, and yet, you're still sitting here, having dinner with them as if it was all a game. As if nothing bad happened, when we all know how fucked up all of this is. You loved Preacher and yet you're allowing this asshole to live. Tell me how odd that sounds."

Preacher shook his head and he saw Robin was close to breaking.

"Excuse me."

Without waiting for anyone to interject, Preacher got to his feet and followed her.

She hadn't gone to her bedroom but to the nursery. She'd kicked off her shoes and stood beside the crib, fingering one of the blankets.

He closed the door and she turned to him, sniffling.

"A really intense dinner, huh?"

"It is."

"I ... I don't know if I can go back down there."

"You don't have to do anything you don't want."

"Like always, it's you who comes to make sure I'm okay. Always."

"They're eating all the dinner. They're loving it."

She smiled but it didn't quite reach her eyes. "You must hate me."

"I can't hate you. I don't know how many times I've got to tell you this."

"Really? You've got your son and the man you've hated more than anything sitting at your table, all because of me. I know you've had difficulty within the club. Am I worth all of this for you?"

"You want me to tell you to pick Reaper? That I don't love you and you can go and be happy somewhere else? I won't follow you for you to live out the rest of your days in peace and quiet?" he asked. "Because I'm never going to want you to do that. I hunted for you day and night. I'm not giving you up, not now, not ever. Not for anyone. You are mine, Robin."

"I don't want you to give me up, but look at us. We're … it's not going to work. Dog's right. You shouldn't want any of them there," she said. "I know you want to hurt them."

"I also know you've got to make a decision here, and I'm not going to take it away from you." It would be easy for him to do so. To kill both Reaper and Bishop, but he didn't want the easy way out. No, he wanted to do the right thing so when he won, Robin would come to him with open arms.

"This is all messed up."

He stepped behind her, putting his hands on her hips and kissing her neck. "Life is all messed up, Robin. The only person who knows what to do next is you. I can wait for you. I've waited for a long time, and I can keep on waiting. I'm starting to realize I'm a really patient guy when it comes to you."

She spun in his arms but he didn't make a single move to touch her. "Why are you so good to me?"

"You're the one for me. Always." He took possession of her lips and she moaned, melting against him.

Gripping her ass, he pulled her close. She didn't fight him. He relished the feel of her soft body against his. In the last few months, she'd started to put some weight on, and he had no problem with her curves. He loved to feel them rocking against his own.

"We need to go and finish dinner."

"I don't like your friend."

"His heart is in the right place, I think. I don't even know if he has a heart but where everyone kept giving up, he didn't. He didn't make me feel crazy for still looking for you. I also don't believe he has a filter between his head and mouth. He just says what he wants to."

She pulled away. "Okay. I can do this. It's not hard, right? We've just got to get through all of this."

"I'll be with you. Remember that. No matter what, you can turn to me. Even with Bethany in your arms." Saying her name finally didn't have the sting he thought it would have.

They walked back down to the table and Preacher was shocked to see no one had killed themselves. It was a success.

****

Later that night, back in the safety of Anne's home, Robin accepted the glass of wine poured for her and giggled as it had to be her third or fourth glass. She rarely drank, if ever. After what Milly did to her, she avoided alcohol. Getting through dinner with Preacher, Reaper, her father, Bishop, and Dog, well, anyone should be entitled to a drink in celebration.

"I thought he was going to stab him or something. You should've seen how tense it was," Anne said. "Your dad kept on asking me a whole load of questions, though. Has he always been so nosy?"

"Nah, my dad and I aren't on the best of terms at the moment. He thinks I'm a whore and well, he could be right. I don't know."

"You're not a whore and the next time I see him, if I ever do, I'm going to slap him. No one calls my bestie a whore."

"But I totally could be." She started to laugh. "I've got two men. I've slept with both and I've got one of their babies, and I can't even think about who I want to keep in my life." The wine was making her loose. "This is the first time I've drank in a very long time. I like it. It feels nice. I've got a bit of a buzz."

"Well, if it makes you feel any better, I'd pick Preacher," Anne said.

"Why would you pick Preacher?" Robin was curious as to why her friend already had a favorite.

"I saw the way he looks at you. Yeah, I know Reaper looks at you a similar way, but this is different." She shrugged. "I don't know. Reaper's look is of … ownership. It's like he has a hold over you and being Bethany's father, I guess in a way, he does, because you both have her together. It's not right the way he does look at you, and it kind of unnerves me. He thinks he already knows how it's going to be with you. Preacher, it's not about ownership, otherwise, he wouldn't have come back to you after the first birth. I learned a whole lot about your life today. Preacher's feelings for you are real whereas I think Reaper, it's not as pure. This could be the alcohol talking."

Anne burst out laughing. "Looking at my own

love life, I could be completely wrong. Robin, you shouldn't be listening to me. I haven't slept with my own husband in years because of what I could possibly catch from him. How pitiful is that?"

"Have you ever thought about being with someone else?" She'd asked Anne this before but wine seemed to make her a little loose in her thoughts.

"Nah, not really. In all honesty, I don't think anyone would want me. It's fine for men. They don't seem to have the same trouble as women. I know he paints me as a monster to the girlfriends. The wife he can't get rid of, but I can handle it. I've been handling it. I've never done anything wrong to him. When I finally fell out of love with him, I was the one who said not to hide it from me, you know. I can deal with the pain. It doesn't hurt now, but I do sometimes think about it. Being with someone else, but then I think about Elijah, and I don't know…"

"It can't be fun living this way."

"The truth is it's not. You know what's worse? When he wants to get laid but there's no one else, he still tries to come to my bed and he wants me. I hate it more than anything. I know I'm second or even fourth in line for his affection. There are times I wish I could make him see what he was missing. I don't love him. Catching your husband with another woman will do that to you. If not the first time, then a dozen times later." Anne sniffled. "I don't want to think about it. I feel like a weak woman when I do."

"You're not weak. You're not even close to being weak, I promise." Robin touched Anne's hand. "I'm thinking you should consider being with others. He's having all the fun, why not you? You deserve it as well."

"Let's not think about it. I don't want to even give myself a chance to think anyone could want me.

A MONSTER'S BEAUTY

Enough about me and my boring old life. Let's get back to what is important, you. Preacher or Reaper. Tell me your thoughts."

"Ugh, do I have to?"

"What stays with us tonight in drink, will stay with us. Huh, that makes no sense."

Robin giggled. "Nothing is supposed to make sense. Okay, fine, let's talk. I love Preacher so much. I spent so much time hoping he'd come and get me, you know. The whole daring rescue. You cannot tell anyone else about all of this."

"I won't. I promise. Stays with us and the drink. I was flattered to be able to go somewhere rather than stick around here and clean."

"I think I should make you go on a date."

"Nah, dating is so not for me." Anne waved her hand in the air. "It's for young people without problems. Now, Reaper, let's talk about him."

Robin finished her glass of wine.

"Why do I feel I'm going to get a lot of dirty details now?"

Robin laughed. "I wouldn't say they're dirty details. More like … scared feelings. When I was taken, I thought Preacher would come. Days turned into weeks, and the whole jargon of how long it took. I was always hoping he'd find me. How hard could it be? Then of course, he didn't ever turn up and I started to lose hope. When you're with someone for so long and your only salvation is being rescued and for that not to happen, it wears on you. He wasn't going to come to my rescue. He didn't care about me, and then I started to have feelings for Reaper."

"Stockholm thing?"

"Maybe, I don't know. We were together and I enjoyed being with him. I got pregnant and he was willing to give up the club life for me. Settle down. I know Preacher would never give up the club life for me. I don't know if my feelings for Reaper are real, or if I've somehow made myself ... open to him. Am I making sense? I don't think I am. I make no sense to myself at all."

"Yes, you're making perfect sense, but it could also be the wine. Let me get another bottle." Anne stumbled out of the room but she didn't stop talking. "I guess what you've got to ask yourself is would you want Preacher to give up the club for you? You know it's who he is. I've only heard all the rumors, but it's part of him, and would you even want him to do something you know he'd hate to do, or risk the club being run by someone who wasn't as good as Preacher?"

Anne came back with the open wine, pouring them both a glass.

Robin gulped the liquid down. She did it so fast, she didn't even taste it. "I've known the club my entire life. I was born into it."

"So, it's not like it's all new for you or anything. It's all the same stuff. The only difference is you're going to be with the president rather than his son. I got a bad vibe from Bishop. I don't like him."

"He used to be great, you know. A good friend. The best person to have around."

"What happened?"

"To put it bluntly, he found his dick, and since then, he's been horrible. Unbearable. I don't know. Maybe it is just me." She shrugged. "The wine is helping big time. There was a time when I'd do anything for him."

"It didn't look that way today."

"I wanted to hurt him. To make him feel the same kind of pain he'd made me feel." Sadness descended on her.

"Okay, so we move on. Nothing can make us moody. Let's lighten the mood. Who's the best in bed?"

"Seriously? You want me to talk about that?"

"I'm not getting any. I know Elijah would but, gross. I don't even know if he bags his dick anymore. Believe me, I have no interest in sleeping with my husband. Not that he lasted all that long." Anne laughed. "How stupid does that sound? You've got to help a girl out here. I bet Preacher's a monster in the sack."

Flashes of Preacher's hands, his mouth, his dick, all of him wrapped around her, consuming her, filling her with all parts of him.

"He's ... amazing."

"And Reaper?"

Thinking about Reaper made her feel guilty. She didn't want to think about her time with him, or even what it felt like.

"You know, I think we both know who you need to pick," Anne said.

"I'm sorry. I ... I'm confused."

"Robin, honey, that excuse isn't going to be able to last much longer. You love Preacher and you think about him all the time. You came back to him."

"But what if I wasn't running to him?" she asked. Her memories had returned. She knew what happened to her when she was taken from Reaper, before she was hit by a car, but what she couldn't seem to access was what was going on through her mind the moment the car hit her.

What was she thinking? Feeling? Did any of it matter?

"And what if you were because deep down, you'd resigned yourself to a life with a man you didn't love but you knew there was no other chance for you? I get it, you know. Staying with a guy for the kids, and I guess I should be telling you Reaper is the guy for you. He's Bethany's dad, and it's only right to have her father in her life. I've got experience with this. It's not ... it's not easy, Robin. You want to know what it's like, it's lonely for the most part. My kids are going to be moving away to college, have families of their own, and I'm going to end up alone with a guy I can't stand."

Tears filled her eyes, and she felt so sick all of a sudden. "I'm going to throw up."

She ran out of the room, toward the downstairs bathroom, and threw up the wine she'd just consumed. Anne was there, holding her hair, and it reminded her of the time she'd been ill with Reaper.

This wasn't the same, though.

What if she didn't love Reaper but she was only staying with him so Preacher didn't kill him?

Was it obligation?

Or love?

For Bethany?

Why wasn't she pushing Reaper aside?

None of her feelings made any kind of sense, and that scared her even more.

A MONSTER'S BEAUTY

Chapter Five

A couple of days later

Preacher made his way to the library where Robin and Bethany were waiting for him. Reaper had finally moved out of his house and was staying at some rented home on the outskirts on the opposite side of town.

He'd never been so relieved in all of his life to finally be rid of the man. It would have been a lot easier if he'd shot and killed him, but he couldn't have everything in life. So he'd settled for just accepting his living and breathing state for now. There was nothing else he could do.

Reaper would be living for some time, and he would have to keep his killing tendencies under wrap. He had moments like this to look forward to. Being with Robin and Bethany, spending time with them. It was why Reaper was still breathing.

Robin walked out of the library, pushing Bethany, and he smiled at her.

"Hey," she said.

"How's the head?" he asked.

Late Sunday night, Robin had called him. She'd been completely and totally drunk and told him about the conversation she had with Anne. He'd never experienced a drunk Robin before, and it had been a revelation. With a few drinks, she was chattier and opened up about a lot of things that were bothering her.

He was starting to like this other woman, Anne. She was on his side, for some odd reason, but rather than question it, he'd accepted it. Anne had his back and she had taken a real shine to Robin. For that, he trusted her and if there was anything she ever needed, all she had to do was ask, and it would be hers. She was more loyal than his own men at the moment, and he needed that.

"It's better. Headaches, no matter how drunk you are, don't last a long time." She rubbed at her temple. "You should have seen Anne though. She looked a little worse for wear this morning."

"You drank a lot."

"Yep. I won't be touching the stuff for another couple of years. So, where do you want to go?"

He took her hand as he moved her out of the way to push Bethany.

"Are you sure you want people in town seeing you so vulnerable?"

"There's nothing wrong with me pushing your daughter," he said. "I intended to be involved with our little girl."

"I can see that."

Once again, their life was held in sadness.

"Don't do that, Robin. There's no need to be sad."

"No need to be sad? Do you even remember what I've done and what we've been through? You've been wanting to kill Reaper for a long time and now because of me, you can't."

"I can. I can kill him anytime I want, and one day, I will, but until then, I'm happy to have you back." He pulled her close, kissing the top of her head, feeling the overwhelming love she gave him filling up his world.

He'd never trusted a woman until he'd allowed himself the chance to be with Robin. He'd killed Bishop's mother because she'd gone to Reaper. Shaking his head, he pushed all of those thoughts aside and instead focused on Robin. She was here and in the now, and he wouldn't be dragged down by any other thoughts or feelings.

"You called her *our girl*," Robin said.

"That's who Bethany is, she's ours."

A MONSTER'S BEAUTY

They walked to a small park. Several people were already enjoying lunch.

A couple of the prospects had set up a small picnic and were waiting for him to arrive. He thanked them, letting them leave so he could have this time with Robin.

After putting the brake on the stroller, he grabbed Bethany, holding her in his arms as he sat down in front of Robin.

"It's nice to see you holding her," she said. "I was worried you wouldn't be able to."

"She's part of you and I love all of you, so I guess I get to love her as well." He smiled at her. "This isn't just a date, Robin, this is something more."

"It is?"

"Yes, I know I haven't been very forthcoming in my reasonings here, and you have to understand I don't want you to end up with Reaper. He's not right for you."

"He's still Bethany's dad."

"I know. But I want to know what happened to you just before you landed in the hospital where Randall was treating you. You're saying Reaper isn't responsible for your shattered foot or broken wrist. I know what I saw, and I want to know how it happened."

It was the one thing they hadn't discussed. He didn't know if it was because of her fear or down to Reaper, or even the revelation of her marriage and Bethany. Either way, he had questions and she was the only one he wanted answers from. Reaper had his own agenda and there was no way he could trust him.

"That time is a little fuzzy. Reaper, he'd gone to the store and he'd taken Bethany with him. I don't know how this group of men found me. Apparently, Reaper owed them a lot of money and they'd been tailing him, I don't know. It's all a little blurry. The details, I mean.

They knew where he lived and when they knocked down the door, I wasn't expecting it. I remember getting hit around the face." She touched her cheek. "On the way down, I hit the counter's edge. It's probably where I banged my head, and then everything went dark. I don't know. I woke up in a cage. Chained to a wall."

She went white as a ghost and Preacher reached out, taking her hand. He needed all these answers even if they did bring back terrible memories.

"It was the most awful experience of my life. I don't..." She stopped and pulled away. She drew her knees up, closing herself off. "I try not to think about it."

"It's fine."

"Why do you want to know about them?"

"When you were in the hospital, I thought Reaper was the one responsible for you being the way you were. The beatings. Then I've since learned he had nothing to do with it, and there was even a chance you were trying to run back to him when you got ran down."

"The men are still out there?"

"Yes. I've spoken to Billy. If there are any details you can remember, anything specific, he's got an artist who can draw the men. I want to know who they are, and I want to hurt them."

"It's dangerous."

"No, it's not. I need to know those men won't come back and hurt you again. I've got to take care of them, Robin. You know this. Do you have any little details at all? Anything you remember?"

Tears were in her eyes and he felt like a bastard for making her relive it all again. This wasn't what he wanted to do, but he couldn't help but think about the men who took her, who hurt her. If he couldn't make Reaper pay, then he'd find someone who could pay the price.

"Then I'll do it, for you. I know this means a lot to you."

"I've got to do something to make you safe."

"Reaper never found them?"

"I don't know. I haven't asked him."

"Maybe I could. It would be easier. That way, you don't have to have any contact with him. I don't want to keep causing you pain."

"I need to know if you love him, Robin. It's something I need to know." He stared at her, waiting, and she didn't speak right away.

"I ... my feelings are all messed up right now. I can't think straight. I know that's not an answer and I'm sorry, but I don't know what to say to make you feel better."

"This isn't about making me feel better. Tell me about what happened," he said. At least he'd be able to not think about all the horrible things she was going through if he could focus on killing.

If Reaper hadn't taken care of the men, then he would.

****

The night Robin was taken from Reaper

"I don't want to leave," Reaper said.

"Then don't. I've got no reason for you to go and you can stay. We've got enough food to last us. Who says you have to leave?" Robin grabbed his arm and kissed him deeply.

In a part of her brain, she was screaming, but she ignored the constant niggle of doubt and worry. Kissing Reaper was the right thing to do. He was her baby's father, and there was no reason for her to not kiss him. It was expected.

Pulling away, he groaned. "I've got to go." He stroked her cheek. "I love you."

"I love you too."

He picked up the car seat and Robin watched him go. He lovingly placed their daughter in the car and she gave him a wave. For a few seconds, he hesitated and she blew him a kiss.

The moment he climbed in and started to reverse out of the drive, she closed and locked the door, leaning against it.

Bethany had been in their world for a couple of months now.

Leaving the door, she felt her shoulders sag. There were times when it was almost impossible to keep it all together. She walked upstairs, but she should have been doing laundry. Instead, she went right upstairs to the nursery.

She'd painted it a pastel pink and had unicorns and all girly stuff within it. Reaper had helped, but he hadn't done anything special.

Stepping inside, she went straight to where there were some baby rompers to fold and put away. The room didn't feel … right.

In fact, in the past couple of weeks, nothing had felt right.

Living with Reaper, she knew he hadn't given up his club, and there was always a hint of nerves whenever she was around him.

The love she felt for him, she questioned it daily. Whenever she had a quiet moment by herself, she couldn't help but think of Preacher. It was easier when Reaper was with her because she would always force those feelings to the back of her mind where they had no chance to shine, but all alone, it was hard.

She couldn't help but wonder where Preacher was, what he was doing. If he'd even forgotten her.

Glancing across the room, she caught sight of her

reflection. Her hair had been dyed per Reaper's demand. This wasn't the first time he'd forced her to change her hair. Whatever Reaper wanted, he got.

Was it because he was growing restless?

Having a baby wasn't all he expected it to be.

She missed Preacher and now, when she was alone, she could give herself a chance to think about all that she'd lost. It was impossible at times, but she dealt with it as she had to. There was no other way for her to deal.

Her life had become little boxes. The first box was her parents. She didn't think about them, but she could imagine her mother laughing about her predicament. When it came to love and affection, Rebecca didn't have it, not even a little bit. She would be loving the kind of pain and indecision she was facing, but that was her mother for her, and she'd come to accept that, not needing to think more about her mother. Bear, he'd made it abundantly clear what he thought of her and what all this meant to him. She didn't have any family left, if she even had any to begin with. Her father wanted nothing to do with her and to be frank, she didn't want to be near a man who thought of her as nothing more than a whore.

Next, Bishop. Her love for him was gone, replaced by an anger she didn't even know she could feel. He'd done this. His own ego had pushed her into the arms of another man, and now, she had a child. Her life was in Reaper's hands every second of every day and she also knew the monster who had taken her could come back. Reaper wasn't a good guy. He'd hurt her in unimaginable ways and she wasn't a fool to think he didn't have some way of hurting her even more.

Then of course there was Preacher. She missed him so much there were times she couldn't think straight because of it. Reaper never mentioned him and she tried desperately not to bring up his name because it always made her hurt inside.

Once again, she was protecting the feelings of another man rather than finding her own feelings. It sucked.

She frowned as she heard the front door click open.

Who would have a key?

None of Reaper's men came to the house. It was part of his request the club stay permanently away from the house so she could have a normal life.

After leaving the bedroom, she made it to the stairs only to scream as two men she'd never seen before ran upstairs. She ran away, trying to go to the bathroom, but they grabbed her by the hair, pulling her back and slamming her against the wall, knocking her out.

****

Pain exploded as Robin opened her eyes to find herself tied up, her hands bound in front of her. She looked around but the pain in her head made her want to throw up.

"Well, well, well, look who's awake. I have to say I thought you'd be out of it all day, and we couldn't have that."

"Please," she said, her voice scratchy. "Let me go."

"No, I'm not done with you yet. You see, I'm going to have fun with you." He used the tip of his blade to run down her cheek and she sobbed as he got to her neck. "So pretty. I've got to have a taste."

He moved between her thighs and it was then she realized her feet were tied, her legs spread open, and the skirt she wore was no protection against this man.

As he climbed on, she screamed.

"Go ahead. It just turns me on even more." He pressed his cock against her core and she gagged.

This didn't stop him though. Even as she begged him to stop and tried to fight. He didn't finish until he was done.

****

The hours passed and the pain was more than Robin could bear. His men took turns to torture her, but the leader, whoever he was, he was the only one to rape her.

They smashed her foot with a hammer, and one man snapped her wrist. They punched and repeatedly kicked her, urinated on her, and when they probably thought she was close to death, they'd leave her shivering with no way to escape.

She thought she could take anything thrown at her. Whenever she felt like giving up, she'd think of Preacher. If she'd been with him, no one would have dared to even approach her.

Was it because of Preacher's power she was attracted to him?

No, she was thinking about Preacher because she missed him. The only reason she was staying with Reaper was because of Bethany, and there was the guilt. Something she didn't want to acknowledge. There was no real competition with her feelings. There was only one man she cared about. One man she loved more than any other, and he was gone, lost to her.

She wondered what he'd do if he saw her now. Would he help or would he let the men finish the job?

Robin started to sob. The intense need to give up was so tangible, it was hard to ignore.

Bethany.
Preacher.
You've got to keep on fighting.

You've got to get back to them.

Just then, out of the corner of her eye, she saw a shard of glass. They'd left her, covered in urine on the floor, and they hadn't cleaned the room. Even as pain flooded her body and all she wanted to do was pass out, she crawled across the floor and grabbed it.

The men were only ever in the room two at a time, at most. Usually, it was just one of them, and they closed the door. Looking around the room, she saw the exit through the window. If they were on the first floor or ground floor, she had a chance.

No matter the pain in her body and the crushing within her soul, she had to get up and do what needed to be done.

Settling on the floor, she closed her eyes and waited.

Could she do it?

This was going to be her only chance.

The door opened and she prayed only one man entered.

As if someone was looking down on her, the door opened and she heard only one voice. The door closed and she was alone.

"Now, now, the boss, he's not here right now, but I've got a thing for broken and bruised women. They turn me on and make me want to fuck like you couldn't believe."

Tears spilled down her cheeks. There was no time for her to panic.

She heard the belt as it opened, and as he came closer, she held the glass within her fist. This was going to be her only chance.

To get out.
To make it free.
To live.

A MONSTER'S BEAUTY

When he came close, she opened her eye, and out of the corner of her peripheral vision, she saw him. Pants around his knees, vulnerable, and he didn't stand a chance. She waited. When he came down close, his hand gripping her neck and pulling her back, she attacked. Plunging the blade into his neck, she watched the horror in his face as he tried to move away. She let out a whimper, but no one would come to her, not with him in the room.

"Wasn't expecting that, were you?" she asked.

He choked on his own blood.

She watched him fall, and again she screamed, letting the sounds of her pain echo around the room so no one would even give a crap to come and look for her.

This was her, all on her own. She didn't have anyone to rely on, just herself.

After he was dead, she stole his shoes and cried out some more as she pushed her shattered foot into one.

Behind the backs of her eyes, she felt the need to vomit, but instead, she kept herself together and knew she had to survive. To finally get out of there alive, or at all.

One.

Two.

Three.

She ignored the sickness and moved toward the window. She put all of her weight on one foot. The shoe helped a lot.

Opening the window, she wanted to sing with happiness. Luck had to finally be on her side. She was on the ground floor and all it took was her sliding one leg out, and then the other for her to be free.

Freedom was within her grasp, and now, all she had to do was keep on running. To keep on fighting for her life.

****

Present day

Robin finished her story, knees pressed against her chest, resting her chin on top of them, and paused as the words stopped. She looked at Preacher, waiting for him to say or do something.

"Then you got hit by the car."

"I got hit by the car."

"Robin, you don't have to keep Reaper around because he's the father of your baby," Preacher said.

"I ... cared about him."

"Do you want to know what it sounds like to me?" he asked.

"What?"

"You made the best of a bad situation. That's not love."

"I don't know what to do anymore," she said, admitting the truth. "Haven't you noticed everything I touch turns to crap?" She gritted her teeth. "I shouldn't be cussing in front of my daughter."

Preacher smiled. "I doubt she'll remember it."

"How can you even look at me right now, knowing everything I've told you before? I willingly went to his bed. I made love to him. We did a lot of things, Preacher." She averted her gaze, no longer wanting him to see.

"Do you love him now?"

She gritted her teeth again but shook her head. There went the guilt again and she looked at Bethany. "Shouldn't I love him?" she asked. "I have a baby with him."

"I know, but just because you have a baby doesn't mean you have to give up your whole life to be with him. That's not how a marriage works, or a relationship."

A MONSTER'S BEAUTY

"Look at Anne. She's staying with a man she doesn't love who cheats on her for the sake of the kids."

"You're not Anne."

"I'm married to him, Preacher."

"And you can get a divorce or become a widow. I can kill him."

"He's been a good father to Bethany even when I wasn't there."

"With all due respect, Robin, you haven't been there for a long time and he's supposed to be a good dad. You don't know what kind of man he is. Who he is with all the bullshit aside."

"Does it surprise you?" she asked. "Him treating me nice, kind, or at all like a human being."

"I have my thoughts with Reaper. I know what he's capable of, and I know deep down there's something I'm missing, but I'll find it. Will you be willing to go to the station? The guy is waiting for us."

She looked at Bethany, and her mind drifted to that time. Whoever those men are, they had to be dealt with. There was no way another woman or any man should have to go through what she did. She'd never been a runner before, but after they shattered her foot, there were times the pain was unimaginable. She'd have to rub it in the dead of night to ease the ache it caused.

Then of course there was her wrist. She never felt confident enough to hold Bethany with just one arm, and she always had to hold her with two. The pain and brokenness of her body aside, they had also interfered with her ability to take care of Bethany. For an entire year, she didn't see her or know she existed. She had thought those men would have been taken care of.

"It was the car," she said.

"What?"

"The car. I remember the rape and torture, but it

was hitting my head on the car that finally closed off my world."

"I imagine the stress didn't help either. You're a beautiful person, Robin. Inside and out. You just don't see it."

She also didn't believe it.

"I want to go with you. Whoever those men are, they have to pay for what they did. Come on, let's go."

Preacher put Bethany back into the car seat as she packed away the picnic. For a few seconds as he was busy, the locked chains on her wrists made her pause. The only ink she wanted on her body and was her own choice was up her chest, beneath her breast. The chains and Reaper's name were forced on her.

"I was held down when I got his name at the base of my back," she said.

She saw him tense as she spoke. Finally, he turned.

She touched the spot she spoke of and his gaze seemed to flare. "The chains meant I was bound to him, and the ink told the world who I belonged to."

"You're your own person, Robin. No one owns you or has a chance of ever taking you away again. I won't let it happen."

She nodded. She couldn't help the sadness consuming her. She believed every word he said. Preacher had no reason to lie to her.

It was all because of Reaper, of her own weakness, and knowing there was no choice.

Reaper, she had loved out of necessity.

The love she had for Preacher was pure. It didn't come from force or a need to keep herself safe. No, the feelings she had for Preacher never went away. For two years, she'd tried to forget about him, ignore him, but he'd kept on coming back, plaguing her thoughts, making her not wanting to give up, not when it came to him.

Even now, she didn't want to let go or give up. For her, it was about being with him for forever.

Bethany made a fuss.

And here was her dilemma. She didn't want to hurt either man. Reaper was a good father and around her, he was a good man. How could she take that away from him when he didn't deserve it?

Pushing all of her thoughts aside, she followed Preacher back to his car and settled into the passenger seat. They drove to the station where Billy was waiting. Without anyone saying a word, she was led back to a room where for the next hour, she talked to a woman who drew what she described.

Robin was able to talk about each man in great detail. The one she killed as well. She even described the glass and the room where she stayed. After each drawing, the woman would hold up the image and she'd point at whichever one it was.

After she was done, Billy shook her hand, and she made her way back to Preacher.

"All done?"

"Yes, can I go home now?" she asked. "Back to Anne's."

"Sure."

He drove her home and this time, when she tried to get Bethany, Preacher helped her, carrying the seat up to the front door.

"I want you to come by the clubhouse next week, if you'd like. I'd like to see you."

"I'd really like that."

Preacher stroked her cheek, stepping closer, and she gasped as he pressed his lips against hers. His tongue traced across her lips, and she gripped his jacket, holding on to him.

"One day soon, Robin, we're going to be happy. You're never going to be sad again and I'm going to give you everything your heart desires."

"That sounds like a promise," she said.

"It is, and every single chance I get, I'm going to make you happy."

"I like the sound of that."

He kissed her again, one final time before pulling away. "I'll call you."

She nodded and let herself in the house. After closing the door, she leaned against it, her heart racing, her lips swollen, her body on fire.

"I don't like that man on my doorstep," Elijah said.

"I'll talk to Anne."

"This is my house. I pay all the bills." She was growing tired of this man. Being with Anne and knowing what a big heart the woman had, it only made her even angrier that this asshole was allowed to do what he wanted.

It had been a long day as well. Talking about the time she was taken, the rape, the pain, it didn't exactly help her feel content or happy.

"Yes, and I've been thinking about that," Robin said. "You see, before I was kidnapped and didn't get to graduate, I was, in fact, a very good student. I had to wonder why you would continue to hurt Anne the way you do, and I finally figured it out. It's not out of some need to be with your wife. The love of her. If you loved her, you wouldn't screw the women you do, and you certainly wouldn't treat her like trash. You two married straight out of high school."

"And your point?" Elijah asked.

"Anne comes from money. You don't. You've

made money, but you're not from wealth. This house is all in Anne's name. With the infidelity, she would not only keep this house, but her trust fund, and also half of your income, not to mention the cost of raising your children and putting them through college. Anne could kick your ass out at any moment."

She shrugged. "I wonder if she knows all of that. She doesn't need you. You're useless as a person, as a man. Instead, like a lot of women, she thinks it's good for the kids to keep you around." Robin paused as she thought about her own feelings when it came to Reaper and Bethany. Her love for him wasn't strong enough.

There was where her problem had been for so long.

She didn't love Reaper. But he hadn't given her a reason to hate him, at least not yet. Pushing all those feelings aside, she picked up Bethany and walked upstairs, waiting for Anne to return. Before she left, she gave Elijah one last parting shot. "Sooner or later, Anne is going to figure all of this out. She doesn't need you. You're nothing but trouble, and the kids, you can see them whenever you want, but she can have a life that's far better than the one you're providing her with."

****

"Where's Robin?" Billy asked.

"As safe as she can be at Anne's house. Do you have anything?"

"I've got some favors and I sent this out to the city big boys to run through. We got a couple of hits," Billy said, spinning the computer monitor so he could see.

He glanced through the list of men all wanted in several murder cases. They all had a list of rape, assault, possession, and priors. Each one part of a gang, a vicious group of men known for hunting easy, vulnerable prey.

Preacher's blood ran cold as he connected the dots.

When he saw the sketched images, he had this vague recollection of knowing them. Now, as he looked at the images on the screen and saw their names, he knew without a shadow of a doubt.

"They're Reaper's men. They work for the Slaves to the Beast."

Which meant if Robin was taken, Reaper was the one to give them the fucking key.

Chapter Six

"She'll need feeding and I've noticed she loves pureed apple and carrot."

"She also likes to eat potato chips. I keep an eye on her and make sure she doesn't choke. You seem to forget I've been taking care of her for some time now, Robin. You don't need to worry."

Robin nibbled on her lip. "You're right. I'm sorry. I'm crazy. I know. You've had her for a lot longer than I have."

Reaper grabbed her hand and pulled her close. "You need to stop stressing out about the small stuff. I know what I'm doing here. Remember, Bethany missed her mother."

She tried not to tense in his arms. Ever since he'd called her the night before while she'd been taking a bath, she'd felt uneasy. Even last night her dreams had been plagued by the first couple of weeks when he'd taken her.

It was like her past memories were fighting with her present ones and they were reminding her she had to remember what Reaper did. He wouldn't hurt her, she knew that. Not now at least, but he had hurt her, and all for the sake of some revenge against Preacher. For so long, she'd been nothing but a means to an end for him.

"I'm sorry."

"No need to be sorry." He pressed a kiss to the corner of her mouth. He'd been aiming for her lips but she'd pulled away and instead, he'd kissed her cheek, nearly.

"I'll be back to pick her up soon, okay?"

"You take as long as you want. Actually, there was something I really needed to talk to you about. When you're done with whatever it is you need to do, you think we can talk?"

"Yeah, of course."

She pulled out of his arms and the moment she took a step away from him, she felt relieved.

"It's Preacher, isn't it?" Reaper asked.

"I don't know what you're talking about."

"Do you think I'm stupid?" Reaper pointed at her. "It's because you're close to him again. I can read your body better than yourself, Robin. I know you've got feelings for him. I know he's part of your life."

"He will always be part of my life, Reaper. Nothing is going to change that."

"No, but I'm still your husband and your child's father. That counts for something."

"I know." The guilt filled her again and she tried her hardest not to show it. "Thanks for taking care of her."

"Anytime. She is my daughter, you know. It's not exactly a hardship."

The longer she was with him, the harder the guilt got. This was totally unfair of her to do this to him.

"I better go."

"Do I get a kiss?" he asked.

She clenched her hands into fists, hoping above everything he didn't see her do it. She stepped up toward him and pressed a kiss to his lips.

He banded his arm around her waist, held her close, and slammed his lips down on hers.

No!
Don't struggle.
Take it.
Don't let him know.

She kissed him back even as her stomach turned and she wanted to throw up. Wrapping her arms around him, she held him close.

"Fuck, Robin, I love you so much."

"I love you too."

It was easier to say the words than walk away. They were lies. There was no way you could love someone and feel this disconnect. Her body rejected him, as did her mind. All she wanted to do was run, to get as far away from him as possible, and try to be safe.

"I can let you go now."

She smiled at him, but as she left the house, she struggled to bat the tears away. If he knew where she was going, she didn't think he'd be so willing to take care of their daughter. She took several deep breaths as she joined Anne at her car.

"You okay?" she asked.

"Yeah, I'm fine. Come on, I hear there's going to be a party and you need to be away from your house." She wouldn't allow herself to think about Reaper. Leaving Bethany with him was hard enough. He'd proven he wouldn't hurt his own kid.

"I cannot believe you're taking me to a clubhouse party. I'm a middle-aged woman and I feel like a rebel."

"You don't have to stop having fun, and you're not that old. I wish you'd stop thinking you were, it's weird. I'm going to be getting to your age and I don't want anyone thinking I'm old."

"Sweetheart, you have no idea what it's like to be me." Anne laughed. "As a mom, you've got to set responsibilities. Your kids look to you to be a role model. I've always put them first."

"And they're not going to see you. I don't know why Elijah gets to walk around town, trashing your name and making people whisper shit behind your back, when you can't have a little bit of fun. The clubhouse won't talk and if your name gets brought up or any mention of what happens tonight, they'll deal with it. They're awesome like that."

"Speaking of Elijah, I have a question. Why is my cheating asshole of a husband being so nice to me?"

"I think he's realizing how special you are and how badly he's treated you." She pulled down the window blind to look at her reflection, applying some red lipstick. She'd never been one for much makeup but she wanted her lips to pop. "Would you go back to him?"

"I haven't left him."

"You've said you haven't been with him intimately. If Elijah swore there were no more women and he'd changed his ways, would you go back to him?" Robin asked.

Anne seemed to think about it, tapping her fingers on the steering wheel. "You know, there was a time I'd have said yes. I mean, I married him because I did love him. The first time I caught him, I forgave him. Obviously, I was upset, hurt and he did some serious groveling to earn back my affection and stuff. I thought I'd done the right thing. Saving my marriage, the choices I'd made. The second one was harder, there was more groveling on his part, and the pain was even more intense. By the time the third one came around, I don't know. I guess he'd hurt me too much and I stopped worrying. By then I knew the signs and I don't know, I just no longer cared. I stopped thinking about him and I guess I started to think about the kids. They will always come first. They have to."

"And you have to forfeit your happiness?"

"My happiness means nothing if you think about it," she said. "I've had my chance and I picked wrong. Elijah was all wrong. We were high school sweethearts and when we did marry, I saw the kids, the house. The love. I thought we were going to be the old couple everyone looked up to, you know? The ones who were together through thick and thin. Our love for one another getting us through the bad times, and strengthening through the good. Now, I see nothing but lies and mockery. Our marriage was never a good one. It wasn't even worth the effort to get dressed up. Did you know he only ever tried for me when we were going to fancy restaurants? If we were going to the movies or hanging with friends, he always dressed like a complete and total slob. All of the other women get the smart businessman. He puts all the effort for them and I get nothing." Anne shook her head. "Sorry, it pisses me off."

"You have a right to be pissed."

"Thank you."

"And the kids still come first?"

"They have to. My situation is not yours, though, Robin. I had my children, and by the time everything was done, it was wrong of me to pull them away from their father. The life I'm living isn't a bad one though."

Robin sat back, thinking about Bethany and Reaper. He was so good with her. As he reminded her, he'd been taking care of her when she didn't even remember she had a daughter.

What kind of mother didn't remember she had a daughter?

"You better not be putting my opinion on your situation," Anne said.

"I have a daughter with Reaper."

"Sweetheart, your life and mine are totally different."

"How so?"

"I married my high school sweetheart. You married the man who kidnapped you and used you in a plot for his revenge. That, my darling, is not grounds for you to stick around just because he's given you a kid. Don't ever compare the two."

"He loves me and he's good with Bethany."

"And you can spend the next fifty-plus years with him when Bethany grows up, goes off to college, and has a man and a kid of her own. You and him alone together. Unless you have more kids as a reason to stay together but there will come a point when it's just the two of you, no one else."

"You're sticking with Elijah and your kids will be leaving the nest as well."

"Again, completely different. I can handle my situation. You don't have to stay with a man you don't love. Don't be miserable." Anne pulled the car into the full parking lot of the clubhouse, turning off the engine.

"You're all for team Preacher."

"And so are you. Don't pretend you're not. You love him and you're only worried about hurting someone else." Anne touched her hand. "Let's stop talking about men. You've brought me here to have a good time and that's exactly what I hope to have. A good time. A very good time."

Robin burst out laughing. "There will be a lot of drink and you're going to see a lot of dirty stuff going on."

"Sex?"

"Possibly."

"Is it wrong how excited I am about that?" Anne said. "I don't mind watching people."

"I don't think I needed to know that."

"Sorry, you're my one and only girlfriend. Elijah was so boring in bed. It's a shock how he's able to keep women satisfied. The guy only knew one position with me."

"I'm now banning you from talking about Elijah. He doesn't get to invade tonight. This is all about you. Come on." She climbed out of the car and she took

Anne's arm in her own. "The guys here are a little crazy but they will respect your word. If you say no, it will mean no."

"And if I don't want to say no and for him to keep going?" Anne asked.

"I didn't hear that."

"Sorry, I'm really excited. I can't seem to help it. The filter in my brain has stopped working entirely."

Robin loved her attitude.

They entered the clubhouse. The music was loud. People were dancing and couples were already making out. They didn't even have to be couples. They were all having a good time and Anne seemed to love it instantly.

Robin was pleased she'd brought her and arranged for Elijah to be the babysitter. In her short time of living with Anne, she'd come to see Elijah took advantage of her way too much, and Robin, well, she didn't like it.

Their marriage wasn't equal and she didn't see why Anne had to be the one who constantly went without while Elijah got to have all of his fun. She'd make sure Anne got just as much attention as her husband, if not, more so. She was looking forward to this.

At the bar, she ordered a couple of shots. She had already spoken to Preacher about making sure Anne had a good time and that the guys knew to take care of her.

Anne downed a shot, letting out a whoop, and Robin followed her, knowing she had limits and wouldn't be adding another.

After Anne had a third, Rider approached and asked Anne to dance.

"Do you mind?"

"Nah, I'm going to go and look for Preacher."

"Do so and you have my permission to be all naughty." Anne winked at her and she laughed.

"Love to."

She watched Anne walk off. She had no doubt the guys would give her an amazing time, Anne deserved it. Moving away from the bar, she came to a stop when she saw her father. She and Bear hadn't been close since her memories or the Reaper revelation. She was a little sad at how their relationship had turned, but there wasn't anything she could do about it. There was no way for her to change what happened. She only hoped in time he'd be able to see she never actually meant any harm to anyone.

"Robin," he said.

"Bear." She no longer felt like she had the right to call him *Dad*.

"I ... it's good to see you."

"I was looking for Preacher. Have you seen him?"

"He's in his office. I ... I'm sorry," he said. "This isn't coming from Preacher or anyone else. I'm not under instructions to be nice to you. You're my daughter and I overreacted. I love you and I don't believe the things I called you. There's no excuse. I hope one day you can forgive me."

"There's nothing to forgive." She wasn't about to hug her father though. The younger her, the less hurt, she'd have run to her father, wrapped her arms around him, and told him they were good. Not anymore.

Bear looked past her to the dance floor. "Do you think she'll accept a dance?"

She looked at Anne and saw her laughing. It was a change to see her be a little selfish and take time for herself. This was probably one of the best ideas she had. "Maybe."

"Robin, I know you say there's nothing to forgive but I remember a time when you'd hug me and I would know it would be okay between us."

"Not everything in life goes away with a big hug. A lot of shit has happened since then. You can't always forget, and sometimes the damage is too far gone. I'm sorry, Dad. I don't know what it is you want from me." She nibbled on her lip. "I ... I need to go and see Preacher." Talking to her dad wasn't on her list of problems to deal with.

Tonight wasn't about having problems, though, it was about having some fun. At least for Anne it was.

Walking into Preacher's office, she saw him standing at the window, looking out over his men. He held a bottle of beer in his hands, and he appeared relaxed. He turned toward her.

"I thought you'd stopped drinking," she said.

"I've come to make an exception. How is Anne?"

"Having fun." She let go of the door and walked closer to him. With every step she took, her body seemed to get even hotter beneath the collar. This never happened with Reaper, not even close. Rounding his desk, she leaned up against it and watched him. "Thank you for arranging everything."

"I promised my guys a bloodbath soon, and a party. They were more than happy to oblige. Besides, Anne is fresh meat to them. You look beautiful."

"Only you can talk about fresh meat and me looking beautiful within the same sentence."

"There's a full stop in there somewhere. It's two different ones," he said. "I can also say beautiful is an understatement. You look amazing."

She laughed.

He stepped up close and she took the bottle from his grip. Tilting it to her lips, she swallowed some of the liquid.

"Why are you here, Robin?"

"You said there was a party."

"Out there is a party. I want to know why you're here, in this room."

"I came to see you."

His fingers danced across her thigh, teasing her. She stared at his lips, wanting them on her.

"I can read your body, Robin, and I know what you want."

"You do?"

"Yes."

"Good." She opened his jacket, putting her hands on his body. "You know, I keep telling myself I shouldn't want you. How I've got responsibilities now and I've got to stay away from you. You're not Bethany's father and I've fucked up everything I've touched so far."

"Then why don't you stop?" he asked.

"I don't want to let you go. I had to live without you for what already feels like a lifetime."

One of his hands gripped the back of her neck, tilting her head back so she'd look at him. His tight grip turned her on even more. This man owned her. The feelings she had, the consuming need rushing through her body. Each day, her yearning for him grew even more, making it impossible for her to focus on anything but him.

She licked her lips, staring at him.

"Tell me what it is you want," he said.

"I want your lips on mine." She moaned as he took possession of her mouth. There was no force or pain, or guilt, just a need. After running her hands up the inside of his jacket, she shoved it off his shoulders and let out another moan as he stepped between her spread thighs.

She whimpered his name. His other hand slid

down her body, cupping her breast, stroking over her nipple before he broke the kiss. "You can stop this at any time."

"I don't want you to stop. Please, Preacher, kiss me."

"I'm going to do more than kiss you."

He grabbed her shirt, pulling it up and over her head and throwing it across the room so it landed in a heap on the floor. Next, he flicked the catch of her bra, her tits falling free.

Robin didn't try to hide as he captured both of her tits, stroking his thumbs across each point before following with his lips. As he licked one nipple, he pinched the other.

"Do you have any idea how much I've missed these tits?" He pressed his face against her chest, kissing, biting, nipping.

She closed her eyes and didn't want him to stop but to keep on touching her. She couldn't get enough. "Please." Running her hands up his chest once again, this time, she pushed his jacket to the floor.

Preacher stepped back, helping her remove his jacket and his shirt. After jumping off the desk, she sank to her knees before him, working on his button and his zipper. He didn't move to stop her as she pulled them down, releasing his hard cock.

When he sprang free, she wrapped her fingers around the length, working him up and down, not wanting to let him go.

He growled. Pre-cum leaked out of the tip and she flicked her tongue at it, tasting it.

She moaned his name again and he suddenly caught her head. His fingers tangled in her hair, holding her in place.

"I don't want you to do this because you feel you

have to," he said.

"I'm not. I'm doing it because I want to, Preacher. I want to suck on your cock."

"Fuck!"

"Don't you want me to?" It was a pointless question. She knew he did.

He didn't force her away from his dick and she stroked the tip with her tongue. Going up and down the vein, she swallowed the head of him. Then she moved down to hit the back of her throat. She pulled up, and then back down.

Bobbing her head, she built up a pace, looking up his body as she tasted him on her tongue. He was exquisite. She'd been thinking about doing this to him. Driving him crazy. Sucking hard on his length. He suddenly pulled her away and lifted her up. He spun her around, pressing her over his desk so her ass was in the air.

He opened her pants, pushing them to her knees, and she remembered the ink on her back.

She panicked and reached behind her. "I don't want you to see," she said.

Preacher leaned over her back and she cried out as he bit her neck, hard.

"Do you think I give a fuck about ink that splays his name? I know who you are, Robin. I know who you belong to and it's not him. They are just words. He doesn't own your heart. I fucking do."

He spread her legs and lifted up. The tip of his cock pressed against her pussy and slowly, he began to sink inside her, going inch by inch until he slammed the last part of him in deep. He gripped her hips, and she couldn't help but tense up as he traced over the name. "This means nothing to me. You're what matters. You and the way you feel about me. Tell me how you feel,

A MONSTER'S BEAUTY

Robin."

"I love you," she said. They were the right words. They didn't leave her feeling sick to her stomach or heavy with regret. Her words had meaning, and they were real.

All of her feelings for Reaper had no real meaning.

Preacher pulled out of her and slammed back inside, fucking her harder, driving in deep.

He was so deep, she truly believed he was in her stomach. The edge of pain and pleasure was so fine she didn't want him to stop and kept begging him for more. She didn't care about anything but what he was doing to her.

Preacher slid his fingers between her legs and started to stroke over her swollen clit. "I want you to come for me. Scream my name, baby. Let me hear it."

He circled her clit, both fingers stroking across, over, and around. Mixed with the feeling of his cock, she couldn't think straight. As she came, she did so with his name on her lips.

It was Preacher, it would always be Preacher. Nothing would ever take him away from her.

He pounded inside her even as her orgasm started to fade but with the pressure of his cock driving in her, she moaned his name, hungry and desperate for more. When he came, she felt his cock pulse, filling her with all his cum, and she loved it.

He nibbled on her neck, biting over her pulse. "I'm nowhere near done with you yet. Tonight, I'll show you who you really belong to."

****

The following morning, Preacher allowed himself the luxury of watching Robin sleep. She was finally his. There was no confusion after last night or during it.

Robin belonged to him, and there was no way he was going to let Reaper take her from him. He knew the truth and now all he had to do was find the right time to show Robin what she didn't know. Reaper had lost her. It was only a matter of time.

After kissing the back of her neck, he climbed out of bed, pulled on a pair of sweatpants, and left his bedroom. He intended to make her breakfast in bed.

Men and women had passed out in the halls and it kind of reminded him of a few years ago, before Robin was taken from him. When he'd allow his men to have fun. Those days were fast returning and as his men saw he was back in charge, not that he'd ever left. But he'd also given them all the update of what had happened. What his plans were and how he intended to execute the Slaves to the Beast.

When he got to the kitchen, he found Anne at the table, nursing her head and drinking from a steaming cup.

"Don't even look at me right now. If my kids could see me, they would be horrified."

"Don't worry. No kids are allowed here. I take it you had fun last night."

"I don't recall ever drinking or dancing so much in my life. I didn't try to sing, did I?" Anne asked.

"No singing that I know of."

"I didn't see you or Robin at all last night."

Preacher raised his brow and didn't say a word.

"You know, I'm rooting for you," she said.

"I know."

"Kill me now," Bear said, stumbling into the room.

"Did you drink a lot last night?" Anne asked.

"I don't drink." Bear slumped into a chair.

"What's your deal then?"

"I don't like to wake up. Mornings are always a challenge for me. Did you have fun last night?"

"Yes, I did."

"Good singing last night," Bear said with a smirk.

Anne groaned. "This is why I should stay away from alcohol. The control I have on myself becomes limited."

Preacher laughed. This was the first conversation he'd had with the woman. He liked her. Of course, anyone who would persuade Robin to pick him was in his good books.

"Where's Robin?" Anne asked. "I haven't seen her this morning."

"She's still sleeping."

"I don't want to know," said Bear.

"Did you apologize last night, like I told you to?" Preacher asked.

"Yes, I even told her I wasn't ordered to do it either."

"Wait, you have to be ordered to apologize to Robin?"

"Look, I've got issues. It's none of your concern."

"You've got issues? That is such a man thing to say, as if it excuses you from actually taking responsibility. You remind me of my husband."

"Do not even think to throw me with that prick."

"Please, he always makes excuses. I'm sorry, my dick just magically appeared in my young secretary. She was needy, baby, she needed me, and I couldn't resist. A man has urges and you can't hold it against me. Ugh, I'm tired of men always making excuses rather than owning up to who they are. You've been an asshole. I don't even know everything you've done to Robin, but I bet she doesn't deserve whatever crap you've said to her."

"This is still none of your concern."

"Actually, seeing as I've adopted her as my new best friend and she seems to have no one but a bunch of men around her, all with an agenda, no mother to speak of, and the last best friend threw her into this mess, I have declared myself as her mother, best friend, protector, and voice. Whatever you say or do, I will find out about, and I'll deal with you."

Anne glared at him. "Robin is a wonderful, sweet, kind, and confused young woman. She's trying to do what's right for her child. It's what any mother would do. All I've ever seen from her is her trying to do right. To help anyone and everyone. I don't know what it is you've done, but if you care about her at all, like a father should, then your apology needs to come from the heart. It certainly doesn't need to be ordered by someone for her to hear it."

Preacher smiled. "I like you."

"I wouldn't. I talk a good talk and I'll be able to help Robin, but when it comes to my own problems, I'm a complete and total failure." Anne laughed.

"Do you think Robin will forgive me?" Bear asked.

"It depends. Do you feel you need to be forgiven? The only way you and Robin can truly come past this is if you really believe you said something wrong."

Bear looked at Preacher.

"No, don't look at him." Anne grabbed his attention, forcing his gaze on her. "No offense."

"None taken." He was finding this thoroughly entertaining. It had been a long time since Bear was put in his place by a woman he hadn't fucked. This had a lot of possibilities. He watched them go back and forth.

"I don't know."

"Well, I think you should understand the entire

situation rather than feeling Robin went out of her way to hurt your good friend. She wouldn't do that. If that had been my daughter, I would've been by her side. She's been through a lot, more than we could've ever imagined. I think you should consider her side of things." Anne got up. "Now if you'll excuse me, I need to go barf."

Preacher got to making his woman breakfast as Anne left to go throw up.

"I wonder if she'll have to line up to barf."

"You need to cut Robin some slack, or better yet, not even bother her with this shit," Preacher said, turning to face his friend with a bowl and whisk in his hand.

"Come on, you can't be serious."

"I'm more serious than I've ever been. Robin doesn't need this crap, not with what we've found out. I need you guys to get in position. If Anne's here, I know Reaper has Bethany. I don't want to prolong this any more than it needs to be."

"What if she doesn't want you to kill him? What then, Preacher? Will you live in harmony with a woman who has a kid with another dad?"

Preacher added a little butter to the pan and then began to add some pancakes. "She won't."

"You don't know this. You don't know shit when it comes to my daughter."

"I know she needs someone strong for her right now and so far, that guy isn't you. Get your shit together, round up the boys, and do as I've instructed. It ends today. I'm not drawing this shit out, not now, not ever. Robin is mine, and once he's dead, you better understand me, Bear, you will never hold Bethany's presence against Robin again."

"You're just going to take her on? Help her grow? Wear your name?"

"Yes." He flipped each pancake before turning to Bear. "That's exactly what I'm going to do."

"She's got Reaper's blood inside her."

"It doesn't make her like him at all. Robin has your blood and Rebecca's. She hasn't turned out like either of you."

Bear burst out laughing. "Really? You think Rebecca wouldn't have gotten into bed with him the first chance she got?"

Preacher stared at his friend. "Your wife sold out the club and your daughter, as did my son. We know Robin went through hell. If you cannot learn to keep your fucking mouth shut, once all of this is done, you can hand in your patch once and for all. I'm done playing games."

"You're fucking serious about this."

"I've never been more serious. You will do this or I'll kill you."

A MONSTER'S BEAUTY

Chapter Seven

Her time with Reaper

" ... five ... six ... seven, eight, nine, ten. You have got all of your beautiful toes. I can just eat you up." Robin picked up her baby girl and pressed her face to her stomach and gave a little growl, pretending to bite, loving the sound of her sweet noises. A baby wasn't supposed to laugh yet and it was always supposed to be gas. Personally, she didn't believe it. She liked to think Bethany was looking at her, smiling, knowing her mother was there to protect her.

"Of course, she's perfect," Reaper said, coming into the room.

The large, angry, fierce biker looked out of place in the nursery room.

She lowered Bethany into her arms, kissing her head, loving her so much. "I never doubted she would be."

Ever since she'd given birth, Robin didn't feel right. It was strange, but her nerves around Reaper had grown. She had a baby to protect now and she was worried he'd hurt her or do something.

Of course, every time she looked at her little girl, she was shot with guilt, thinking about Preacher. They should have gotten the chance to experience this. To know love, to hold it and keep it.

Only, they'd lost it, never being able to nurse a baby themselves.

"You've gone all sad on me again," Reaper said, sitting on the floor.

"It's nothing. Just thinking thoughts, you know how I get."

"Yeah, well, the only person I can figure who'd make you sad and miserable is Preacher, so I guess you're thinking about him."

Robin hated to lie. It wasn't that she was bad at it, but when lies started to build, they spread, and before anyone knew what was happening, one tiny lie became a thousand, and an entire life could be ruined and destroyed because of it. No, she wouldn't lie to him.

"I was. I was thinking about our little girl, you know. It's nothing bad or anything."

"Do you think about him and your kid?"

"Sometimes. Not all the time. With Bethany here, I don't think about much anymore. She is the cutest, sweetest, most beautiful girl in the entire world." Her voice had changed to that of a baby's as she talked.

Reaper laughed. "I think it's time for us to put her down for her nap."

Robin didn't want to let her go. But if she didn't get her sleep, she'd be cranky, and in that, she had no choice. Getting to her feet, she placed Bethany in the crib. She'd already changed her diaper and had done all the necessary preparations to put her to sleep. "You're going to sleep now and when you wake, I'll read to you." She leaned down, kissing her already sleeping daughter's cheek. "I'm starting to think she only likes my breasts for the milk she can get." She pouted. "Once she's done with me, she'll toss me aside."

"I wanted to get back to working on your training again," Reaper said.

She grabbed the baby monitor, pulling the door so she wasn't closed off. "More training? I thought I did all of this months ago."

"You were also pregnant and I don't want to see you ever caught off guard."

"You know, I've heard a kick to the balls is very productive." She hated it when he forced her to train to take down an opponent. "Besides, with you around all the time, you're going to be able to protect me."

"As you know, there will be chances along the way when I get sloppy."

She put her hands to his chest. "No, how dare you even think you can be sloppy."

Reaper pressed her against the wall at the bottom of the stairs. Her instinct to recoil was strong but she didn't. She held onto her composure, keeping her shit together as he stared at her, waiting.

Tilting her head back to look him in the eye, she smiled. "Are you sure you want to train?"

"I want you to be ready for anything. Come on." Before she could protest, he led her out to their very secluded front yard. Unless it was one of his club men, they never had any visitors. No one ever came to find them.

Since moving in, Reaper hadn't left her alone and he'd also disconnected all the phones as well. Her way of getting in touch with the outside world had been lost to her, but she knew it was his way of trying to take care of her. A part of her knew he was also acting on the way she'd been treating him. She hadn't been the same since Bethany was born and she didn't know why it scared her so much.

With the baby monitor resting on one of the porch steps, she turned to Reaper. "You know stress doesn't help the production of milk."

"I'm not wanting you to spray any potential attacker with your tits. I want you to be able to defend yourself."

"Okay, you're the boss."

For the next hour or two, he showed her moves and methods to get out of certain poses and attacks. Each one scarier than the last. By the time they were done, he'd told her where to attack to get the most impact, and what could be used. She didn't like all this additional knowledge. Especially for fear she might use it on Reaper. What if she did attack Reaper at night?

Killed him.

What would she do then?

Could she even go back to Preacher?

Was there a way for her to find happiness with the man she loved while also raising another man's child? It seemed way too far-fetched.

"Are you still in contact with Bishop?" she asked as Reaper lifted her up in the air, spinning her around.

She saw the anger in his eyes before he let her go. "Yes."

"Does he know where you are?"

"If you're wondering where Preacher is, he's still looking for you."

"No, I didn't mean that."

"Then what did you mean?" he asked. His voice was harsh, growling.

"I don't know. I guess with Bethany, it reminds me of the friendship we lost."

"Well, if you cared so much about him, you wouldn't have screwed his dad."

Robin tensed up in his arms. She pulled away from him but Reaper grabbed her. "You're hurting me," she said.

"No, I'm not. You're just afraid I will hurt you and you don't need to be. You're the one who has changed, Robin. Not me. I would never hurt you or Bethany. I love you both and I know you're having doubts. I don't blame you. You're afraid of me, and I do get it, but I'm telling you that you don't need to be afraid. I would never do anything to harm you or our child. I love you with all of my heart."

Before she could say anything else, the monitor

alerted them to Bethany waking. "I better go see her." She wanted to say more but instead, she turned on her heel and left, going to attend their daughter.

Reaper's anger scared her. She was also afraid of her own feelings. What had happened to her? This was her life now. She needed to settle and get used to it. Reaper had been good to her. Not in the beginning, but now he was.

Only, this had all been about revenge to him. His love for her wasn't pure. It wasn't anything. He'd wanted to hurt Preacher. If he was still in contact with Bishop, did that mean he was sending photos and updates about how they were doing? Did Preacher already know she was mother to his enemy's child?

Lifting Bethany in her arms, she smelled the diaper and immediately started to change it. If he knew the truth, was that why he wasn't coming to her? Coming to get her, to find her, to love her.

Could anyone really love her now?

She'd been in bed with the enemy and it hadn't been by force.

Tears filled her eyes, but she swatted them away. She didn't want Reaper to know the full extent of her fears and concerns. This was supposed to be about them having a fresh start, not her craving the love of another man. She had to cut everything off from her old life if she was ever going to be able to survive this.

Bethany needed her.

Preacher didn't.

All she had to do was survive. If there was ever a chance of her to be with Preacher again, she'd take it, but would he ever willingly accept another man's child?

It wouldn't matter. The option would never arise.

She would just accept what her life had been dealt. Some women were in a much worse predicament than she was.

****

Present day

"Breakfast in bed. What did I do to deserve this?"

"Nothing. I want to surprise you."

"I can't believe this is happening to me. I'm so happy."

"Good, I want you to be nothing but happy."

She giggled and took a bite of the food. "This is so good. I love your pancakes." She took a sip of her coffee and again another moan. "I'm spoiled. I know I am."

"You're loved."

"Yay, I love you too." She put her fork down and reached over, kissing him. "Have I told you that recently?"

"Not enough."

"Then I love you. I love you so much."

"Once we do this, I want you to get dressed so we can head on over to Reaper's. I need to talk to him about something."

"Something? Is it bad?"

"It's not great, but it's not something you should worry too much about."

"Worrying seems to be where I come from these days." She felt a twist within her stomach. "Are you angry with me?" she asked.

"I've got no reason to be angry with you. Why would you even think that?"

"Bethany and Reaper. I can't regret giving birth to her, even though it was in a car. Not exactly in a bed with Randall guiding me through it. It was a crazy time."

Preacher took her hand. "We're going to have more kids and I'm going to love Bethany as if she was my own. You know that, right?"

"Yeah, I know. I wanted to talk to you about Bishop actually," she said, pushing some hair off her face.

"What about him?"

She smiled. "I expected you to be closed off and tell me you didn't want to talk about your son."

"Do you want me to growl at you a little, scream?"

She chuckled. "No, I think this is easier. I hope it's easier." She licked her lips. The pancakes held no appeal as her stomach tightened. "I'm not stupid. I know the rules of the club when it comes to traitors. My mom, a couple of the guys, Bishop's mother. They all had to be taken care of."

"I know."

"But what if you made an exception for Bishop?"

"Robin, if I let Bishop live, I will look weak."

"I … I'm angry at him. I don't know if I'll ever get over what he did or even why he did it, but I don't want him to die." She didn't want to have his death on her conscience. "I shouldn't ask you. I know. I bet the club has had enough of dealing with me."

"They will always do as they're told."

"But that doesn't exactly help my cause, does it?"

"Are we talking about your dad now?"

"My dad. The club. Everyone. I don't want people to hate me."

"They won't."

"How do you know that?"

"I don't know that. I don't know what the fuck is going on in my life half of the time. Look, Bishop will be dealt with as part of club business. He made his decision and there's nothing I can do to change that."

He stroked her cheek. "It's time for you to stop worrying about everyone else. Bishop threw you under a bus, and you've been picking up the pieces ever since. Don't let his mistakes be yours."

"I've got plenty of my own."

"Don't do that." He leaned forward and kissed her. "Are you done with breakfast?"

"Yeah, I don't think I can eat another thing."

"Get dressed. I want to take you to Reaper's. We'll pick up Bethany and then go to the park or something. Would you like that?"

"If you can do that. Are you allowed to do that?"

"Baby, I can do whatever the hell I want. I don't answer to anyone."

She climbed out of bed, no longer caring about her nakedness, grabbed his face, and kissed him. "I love you."

"Not as much as I love you."

This was what she had hoped her. What she once prayed for.

Were all of her dreams finally being answered? She stepped into the bathroom and caught sight of her reflection. Her face was a little older. The ink on her body a constant reminder of what happened to her.

The ink crawling up the side of her body with the roses, that was all her, but the cuffs around her wrist and Reaper's name… All of that had been part of his plan to hurt Preacher. Was Preacher hurt every time he saw them, or did he not care like last night when he took her?

Pushing all of her doubts aside, she instead focused on just getting ready. She took a quick shower and changed into some clothes. Preacher still had some of her old stuff in his closet and she pulled on a pair of jeans and a loose-fitting top.

She left her hair down, and she'd only dried it with a towel so there were damp spots.

Preacher had already taken her plate down and

made the bed, and he was waiting for her at the main clubhouse. She didn't allow herself to look in any direction. Anne was waiting for her at the door.

"Are you okay to drive?" Robin asked.

"I am. I just wanted to see you before I went. Last night was a total blast. I loved it, and thank you." Anne pulled her in for a hug. "Preacher has already told me you've got some business to take care of. I'll see you later, maybe? You think that will be fine?"

"Yeah, of course." She held her friend close before watching her drive away. "Thank you for allowing her to have some fun."

"A friend of yours is a friend of mine. We're taking the car," Preacher said. He opened the passenger door for her and she climbed in. She noticed he was checking his phone and typing a message.

"Anything important?"

"Just the guys."

"Can I help?"

"No, it's nothing to worry about." He pocketed his cell phone and she tried not to think about how quiet and secretive he was being. This wasn't like Preacher, at least not recently unless he was hiding something. Rather than worry, she looked out of the window and Preacher put on the radio.

Something was going down today. She didn't know what it was, and her nerves took on a whole new level.

Was he doing one of his drug runs? Guns? She wasn't a fool. Her mother had told her from a young age what it was her father and the club did. At first, she'd been so embarrassed, and she'd hated to even think about it, but now, she accepted it. She didn't want a part in any of it. Drugs were something she never wanted to dabble in and guns, she hoped no one ended up dead. A stupid way to hope, but it was one that had gotten her through many a dark time.

They arrived at Reaper's house and her hands shook a little. That she knew of, this was the first time Preacher had come to Reaper's.

Both men once again together. They had lived together for a short time before Reaper got this place. Again, she didn't ask how he got it, only that he now owned it, and she always felt a lot of stuff wasn't her business. This wasn't her life and it wasn't her job to keep an eye on every single man in her life.

She took a deep breath, let it out, and did the same thing over and over again, trying to hide how sick she felt. The pancakes threatened to spill back up but rather than give them a chance, she climbed out of the car and simply breathed in deep, hoping to calm the fear filling her body.

Reaper opened the door. He held Bethany against him.

She smiled at seeing her little girl, rushing toward them.

"Hey," she said. "How was she?"

"She's been perfect. I thought you were spending the night with Anne," he said. "Having a girls' night."

"Yes. I did. Preacher brought me back. I went to the clubhouse with Anne last night."

"I see."

She didn't like his tone and he stepped away, still holding Bethany.

"I, er, I need to use the bathroom," Robin said.

This wasn't good. Reaper was angry. She instantly wanted to make him feel better. To soothe the monster so he wasn't hurt. Taking a deep breath, she waited.

"You know where it is."

A MONSTER'S BEAUTY

She had to get some distance.

Without looking back at Preacher, she quickly escaped to the bathroom. After closing the door behind her, she leaned up against the counter, pressing her head to the cool tile. "You can do this. It's not your problem he's upset."

In and out.

Deep breaths.

Don't rush.

She didn't have a problem. Reaper did. This wasn't her fault.

It is your fault. You told him you loved him. You were willing to make a life with him. Now you've got to deal with the consequences. You don't get to have a happily-ever-after. They're for people who deserve it. You're nothing but a whore and a slut. Who would sleep with their best friend's dad? Who would fuck the man who took them? Someone sick and twisted, that's who.

She splashed cold water on her face, ignoring the pain in her temples. This wasn't the time or place to be listening to her scary thoughts. She had to get control of herself and not get lost in the pain.

When she no longer felt like she was going to throw up, she opened the door and closed it behind her. She wore sneakers, so they didn't make a sound as she walked across the room, heading back to where Reaper and Preacher were talking.

"You know, I find it interesting you're still sniffing around her," Reaper said. "I'm the father. I'm the one with the kid. Robin belongs to me. You've got to admit defeat."

"You think you've won her?"

"Look where I am. You've got to understand, Preacher, she will always return to me. Bethany is my flesh and blood. Did you know I got her to admit she loved me? Robin is mine, and you lost her. All this time, you trusted all the wrong people."

"Then why did Robin come to me last night? I find this all fascinating. You took Robin not because you wanted her; no, that came later. You took her so you could hurt me. When it comes to my woman, your feelings are all about hate. It's what you can get out of it, not what you feel for Robin."

"I love Robin."

"No, you don't."

Reaper laughed. "And you're an expert?"

"Did you know Robin got a good look at the men who attacked her? She told me all about it. How you were going out to the store or something with Bethany. All a very convenient way to make sure Robin was alone. It was all just a little too perfect how they were able to enter your home, take Robin, and you didn't have a clue."

Robin's body went completely cold.

Preacher continued. "You see, I took Robin to Billy. You know, the guy in charge, and he had one of those sketch artists. We were able to run the images from her memory through his computer and you know what we found?"

Reaper didn't say anything.

"I know those men and I know they're your boys. The only way they could have gotten to Robin was if you let them. If you gave them the motherfucking key to your house. They would be under your instruction the entire time."

No, this couldn't be happening.

"You can't prove anything." Those were Reaper's words. No denial. No nothing. The pain, the soreness, it was his fault. He had hurt her even worse than she could have imagined.

Tears flooded her eyes.

Pain.

Anger.

Hatred.

All of it combined to make her shake. "It's true," she said, stepping out from the shadows where she'd been standing.

Reaper whirled around. "Robin, what are you doing there?"

"You sent those men to hurt me?"

"Preacher doesn't know what he's talking about."

"I just heard everything!" she screamed at him. Bethany started to fuss. She rushed toward her daughter. While Reaper was likely trying to figure out whatever lie would get him out of this, she grabbed her baby and took a step back. The tears already fell thick and fast. She felt sick, alone, lost. This couldn't be happening to her, and yet it was. There was no getting away from what he'd done and was going to keep on doing. "You sent those men to hurt me."

"Robin, I had to."

"You had to get them to beat me up? To rape me? Did you know they were doing that? Did you know they pissed on me and laughed as they did? They shattered my foot, and there are nights I lie awake because the pain is still there. I will never fully recover from what they did to me and it was all you. You did it? How could you do that to me?" she asked.

"Why did you do it?" she sobbed.

"Look at you, Robin. You still have the stench of Preacher on your body. You think I didn't see what was happening to you? You wanted him back. Having my baby didn't change anything."

"This was to punish me for having feelings?"

"No," Preacher said. "This was so he could be the

one to rescue you. Those men were expendable, right? Are they still alive or did you kill them?"

She kept looking at Reaper but she couldn't believe it. "Do you know how guilty I felt for having feelings for Preacher? It wasn't easy for me. I didn't know what to do and you nearly had me killed to be a hero. A good man doesn't hurt the woman he loves just so she can fall in love with him. I can't … I won't…"

"Robin, please," he said.

"No, don't talk. Don't even try to tell me anything. I don't want to hear you. I don't want to even acknowledge you. I hate you more than anything right now." She held Bethany close to her.

"I'm her dad. You can't take that away."

"No, she doesn't have a father," Robin said. "You will never be good enough to be her father."

She felt sick. "Preacher, would you please drive me back to Anne's?"

****

After dropping Robin and Bethany back with Anne, Preacher drove back to where he'd left Reaper. He didn't tell Robin about what he had planned. He had to wonder if she even knew what he was going to do or if she wasn't thinking that far ahead. Either way, Reaper would be taking his last breath.

Parking his car, he saw Dog sitting on the porch steps, smoking a cigarette.

"You know those are going to kill you," Preacher said, climbing out of his car. His cell phone rang and he accepted Bear's call.

"They're dead," Bear said.

"Burn the bodies and bring it to the ground. I want Slaves of the Beast to be nothing more than a faded memory." He ended the call and looked at Dog. "Did he do anything?"

"Nope. I may have gotten a little handsy with the knife, but I didn't think you'd mind me playing slash with him."

Preacher didn't ask any more questions. He walked in to find Reaper still tied to a chair. His face was covered in blood and his body had lines from the knife. It had torn through fabric and flesh.

Preacher grabbed another chair and pulled it close.

"Your men are dead," he said. "Every single little piece of scum. They're all gone."

"You can't kill out the name. You can try, but you'll always fail, Preach. You don't have it in you. There will always be Bethany."

"This guy is a piece of work," Dog said.

"Yeah, he doesn't seem to get that he lost."

"I didn't lose. You kill me, then what are you going to tell Bethany?" Reaper asked. "She's my flesh and blood, and no matter what I did, you can't wipe me out."

Preacher smiled. "Actually, she's at the age no one remembers. You see, Reaper, your little girl is going to call me daddy. I'm going to raise her like she was my own. She'll be a Twisted Monsters MC brat, and you won't even be a memory. You'll be nothing."

"She won't let you do that. Robin won't let you."

"You sent your boys to hurt her. You didn't play out your daring rescue. There's no way she will ever trust you again. You're finished. The moment you set your plan in motion, you lost her, and we both know you never had her, not truly. She's just a means to an end for you, but now you've lost her."

"You're not going to do this. She loved me. She told me so."

"You took her from me. You raped her, beat her,

and tried to make her fall in love with you. You failed at all of them. Robin is mine. She will always be mine and there's no way I will ever let you take her from me." Preacher slammed his fist into Reaper's face.

"She'll know you killed me."

"I don't care. I don't take orders from a woman. I'm doing this for Robin and after what you did, there's no way you deserve to walk on this earth." He continued to slam his fist into Reaper's face. When he was worried he'd pass out, he asked Dog for a knife. The first piece he took from him was the cock that he'd used to impregnate Robin. He tore it off his body, and in front of him, cut it into pieces so there was no chance of ever using it again. Not that Reaper was making it out of this house alive. No, Preacher wasn't taking that chance.

It was all over for him and he wasn't going to allow him to get away, or to live, or to have anything. He was dead. Cold fucking dead.

With his dick gone, he took his fingers. Piece by piece, he took from Reaper until he was screaming, begging, and asking for forgiveness. Preacher didn't grant it. He took his tongue, his nose, his eyes, and when he was done, he finally slit his throat.

He was covered in blood and Dog stood back, watching and witnessing it all.

Finally, he removed his clothes and took a shower. Dog was waiting with a fresh pair of clothes and a large tub of gasoline.

Once he was dressed, he opened the gas and began to pour it over the man who'd been his enemy. He should've done this a long time ago, and right now, he couldn't think of a single good reason why he hadn't killed Reaper. If he'd taken care of this business, Robin never would've been taken. She would've been safe and he wouldn't have had to deal with the potential fallout it had caused.

After he lifted a match, he threw it onto the body and he and Dog left the house. They leaned up against his car, and this time, Preacher took a smoke from him.

"Damn," Dog said. "Remind me to never get on your bad side."

"He had it coming."

"I don't know. I think the coldest thing you did there was cut off his dick and then keep on cutting it. Cold, so fucking cold."

"He didn't need his dick anymore."

Dog burst out laughing. "We both know he wasn't getting away yet you still continued to do it."

"He hurt my woman with that thing. There was no way I was going to let him keep it." He took a long deep draw on the cigarette, waiting for the satisfaction of what he did. He didn't have anything.

No happiness. No nothing. Just an emptiness.

He wasn't happy, nor was he sad. He was nothing. There was just nothing to him.

The house started to catch fire.

He and Dog stayed there. He'd already called Billy to wait for his signal. When he was ready, the fire crew would come, but until then, there was nothing.

"What happens now?" Dog asked.

"I hear you're looking for a couple of extra fighters."

"Are you back in the game?"

"It's time to get back in the game." He'd taken care of this little problem and now he had to wait and see what it would be like with Robin before he approached her. This was the risk he'd taken, but he'd done it for her.

Running a hand down his face, he climbed in the car with Dog by his side and phoned Billy. The house was done for. He let him know to send his boys to put it out within an hour.

A MONSTER'S BEAUTY

Chapter Eight

No one was able to identify the body, but Robin knew who it was.

The fire had been the talk of the town, which lasted for a month. Now, it was nothing more than a faded memory. She put the latest batch of books onto the shelf and pushed the cart around the library.

She was numb.

It was strange. She didn't feel upset, but Reaper had been part of her life for nearly four years. Bethany was nearly two years old and growing up so fast. Anne was taking care of her at the front desk. They'd bought a small crib with a couple of toys to keep her entertained. She still lived with Anne.

She hadn't seen Preacher since that day. He hadn't stopped by, neither had her father, and she hadn't gone to the club.

He'd killed Reaper and now he wasn't even coming to see her. Was this his final way of saying it was completely over between them? She didn't want to think about what it could all mean.

With her empty cart, she walked back to the desk where Anne sat typing away at the computer.

"Hey," she said.

"So, I was thinking you could go to the diner and get us some lunch. I'm finishing up the order and I'm getting hungry. I've got Bethany, no need to worry."

"You'll keep an eye on her?" Even with Reaper gone, she didn't want to let her baby out of her sight. She didn't know if Reaper had any enemies or long-standing friends.

"I'll keep an eye on her."

"Okay, then." She took Anne's order and left the library. She kept trying not to think. As she passed a couple of people, they stopped to say hello to her. She didn't make small talk and rushed toward the diner. On her way inside, Bear was coming out. "Sorry," she said, stepping out of his way.

"Robin."

"Bear."

At that moment, she missed her dad more than anything else. She wanted to hold him, to ask him if everything would be okay, but she didn't. Instead, she bowed her head, waiting for him to go.

"I'm glad I ran into you," he said. "I'd like you and Bethany to come to dinner."

"Bethany?"

"You know, my grandkid," he said.

This made her look at him. He'd never acknowledged Bethany as his.

"I've been thinking about her a lot lately and you know, I don't want her to hate me as a grandad. I know I've been an asshole a lot lately, and well, I would like us to get to know each other again, as a family."

"Oh."

"If that's okay with you. I know I fucked up a lot and I want to make it up to you."

"Yeah, of course. I would like that too."

He smiled. "How about this Sunday? You, me, Bethany, you come and we have a family dinner."

"I'd like that." The family dinners at Anne's were rather tense. Elijah wasn't happy with his wife's newfound freedom. She no longer waited around for him or asked his permission. She lived her own life and didn't need him for her to be happy. It was nice. She even believed Anne had found someone.

There were secrets her friend kept, and she didn't have a problem with that. It had been a long time since Anne had looked happy, at least from what people had told her.

Entering the diner, she felt a little happier.

It wasn't going to be the same with her father, she knew that. They had too much bad blood between them, but that didn't mean they couldn't find a way to make it work, for Bethany and for themselves.

She ordered two lunches and stood waiting for them.

The diner was noisy and she looked around to see all the different people in conversation, enjoying their lunches.

Did Reaper beg for his life?

Why didn't Preacher ask her?

What was she going to tell Bethany?

Her daughter didn't show any signs of missing her father, and Robin felt guilty. Why did she feel guilty? She didn't care. After learning the truth of what he did and what he organized, there was no way she could feel anything for him. He'd gone out of his way to hurt her and rather than protect her, he'd thrown her into hell all because he wanted to be a hero.

She was handed her food and she took it with a smile. Leaving the diner, she started to walk back to the library. It was the same routine day in, day out. She could go through her life with her eyes closed it was the same basic, monotonous tasks.

Her life was so different now than before she'd been taken, even during her period of kidnapping. Some things remained the same, though. She still hadn't graduated high school and that was something she wanted to do, to have some kind of goal in life, to know what she wanted.

Across the street, she stopped as she caught sight of Preacher. He was looking right at her as he came out of the station, Billy beside him.

Did he hate her?

Was he going to ignore her?

Rather than wait for his rejection, she quickly rushed toward the library.

This is stupid, Robin. Why are you running?

"Robin!" Preacher called her name.

She kept on walking even as she screamed at herself to stop. To listen to him. She was too stubborn, and rather than give in to him, she kept on moving.

When she got to the entrance, Preacher had caught up with her. He captured her arm, stopping her.

She spun to face him. "Preacher, hi. How are you doing?" she asked, forcing a smile to her lips. This was scary after everything that had happened. He knew what Reaper had done, why he'd done it. Her life, her feelings, it had all been a big game to Reaper. He hadn't cared about her at all and she did find Reaper a little scary.

"You heard me shouting for you."

"Oh, you were shouting for me? Sorry, I didn't even realize. I was busy, you know, and hungry."

"You're babbling."

"It's what one does when she doesn't know what to say." She didn't even know why she was still talking. "Are you done? I want to go and have lunch. You know, stare at my daughter."

"We need to talk. I want you to come to my place tonight."

"Wow, dinner with dad and now seeing you," she said. "I wonder what I did for it to be my lucky day?"

"Why are you being a bitch? It doesn't suit you."

"Why has it been nearly two months since you killed Reaper for you to come to me?" she asked, firing him back a question. "You come here, ordering me around, and you expect me to follow you? You expect me to do as I've been told, huh?" she asked.

"Robin, it's not like that."

"I have to wonder if you'd have even given me a thought if you hadn't come to see Billy and saw me. I was more of an afterthought, wasn't I?" she asked.

"No."

"You're lying. You know what, I'm sick and tired of liars. I've got no time for you or for this." She tried to pull away, but Preacher wouldn't let her go and it only made her even madder. "Let me go."

"I've wanted to come to you but I've had club shit to deal with."

"And that always comes first. Have you killed Bishop now as well?"

"Are you pissed I didn't ask your permission?"

"Why didn't you?"

"Because I wasn't going to listen to you or your fucking guilt. It's what you're good at, right? Feeling guilty? He sent men to hurt you on purpose and if you think I was going to let him get away with it, you're wrong."

"That wasn't your choice to make."

"Robin, I love you. You're my entire world and I nearly lost the club because of my obsession with finding you. I'm not an easy man and I'm not going to let someone who willingly hurts you walk. Reaper had to die and I made sure of that. I took care of it, like I should have done the moment you turned up."

Tears filled her eyes. "Then why didn't you come and find me? Is it … over?"

"No. It's not over." Preacher pulled her into his arms. "It will never be over. Not with us. I love you too fucking much and I can't bear to see you like this."

Without any reason at all, she began to sob. "I'm sorry."

"You've got nothing to be sorry about."

"I don't know why I'm crying."

"I do. It's fine. You can mourn him."

She shook her head. "This isn't about him. It hasn't been about him for a long time. I don't love him. I don't think I've loved him ever. I'm so confused. I'm sorry. I shouldn't have been a bitch. I don't know what to do. After finding out what he'd done and then you hadn't come and seen me, I thought you were through with me. I don't know what to think or how to feel anymore. It's all messed up."

Preacher stroked her cheek and kissed her head. "I think you should come to my place tonight. Bring Bethany with you." He kissed her again. "I won't hurt you."

"What do I do?" she asked.

"If you're willing to hear me out and give us a chance, you'll be at my house tonight. If not, I'll know you want nothing more to do with me." He nodded past her shoulder and Robin turned to see Anne. She gave Preacher a wave.

"Love you, Robin."

She didn't say anything. He kissed her and walked away. It was on the tip of her tongue to beg him to come back, but she didn't. She turned and walked into the library.

"Bethany's asleep. She is such a delightful little girl," Anne said.

"She really is. I don't know if the food is cold. I'm sorry. I tried to get here as soon as I could."

"I saw you with Preacher. Why do you look like you're going to cry?" Anne asked.

Robin took a deep breath. "I'm not going to cry. I'm ... I don't know what I am, to be honest. My emotions have been all over the place with everything."

"Preacher's there for you. I know you're having a

hard time, but he loves you. You can see it." Anne opened up her meal, picked up the burger, and took a large bite.

Robin laughed. "I thought you were dieting again. Some kind of carb thing?"

"I've decided all diets suck. Nope. It's why I sent you to lunch at the diner. I'm happy with the way I am. I've had a couple of kids. There's no way I'm ever going to be a size zero, not that I ever was. If men can't stand a woman with curves, then I can't stand them."

"You've changed your opinion."

"Screw Elijah and everyone else who doesn't like me. I'm sick and tired of trying to fit into the mold. You've helped me to see this, Robin, you have. I couldn't have done it without you."

Robin picked up a fry. The conversation had taken a dramatic turn. "Really? How?"

"Everything you've gone through. I haven't lived it or anything, but you've been through a whole lot and you're still standing."

"I'm barely getting by. I live with you. My husband is gone. My best friend is nowhere to be found, and that was the first time I spoke to the guy I do love, and I feel awful."

"You keep on fighting. For yourself, for Bethany. Even when you didn't have your memories and they all came back, you were strong. You're a strong woman, Robin. You're not falling apart. You're braver than you realize."

"I'm not the kind of woman you need to make a role model out of, Anne. I *am* falling apart. I'm not good, not even close." She felt the tears already welling in her eyes. How could Anne even think she was strong? She'd never been strong. There was nothing good about her, or what she felt. She was a mess. Look at the decisions she'd made from Reaper, to well, Reaper. He'd been a big mistake, even if she did have Bethany, he'd been the worst part of her life.

Anne took her hand. "You're not falling apart and even if you do, I won't think less of you. In fact, I hope you do, it will make you seem more like a human than a robot."

She laughed. "I'm not a robot. If I was, this wouldn't hurt so badly." She sniffled. "I'm sorry."

"No, cry, but … did you and Preacher, you know?"

"Did Preacher and I what?" she asked, frowning.

"Your emotions are all over the place. You don't seem to be able to hold one thought. You're crying, and if I wasn't mistaken, last night I watched you smear peanut butter on a boiled egg."

"So?"

"Have you thought about the fact you might be pregnant?"

"No, that's not possible. I can't be pregnant."

"Why not?"

"Because now is so not the right time and there's no way I can do all of that right now. No, it's not possible." She couldn't think about being pregnant right now.

Anne continued to look at her.

"No, it's not. I mean, I know I haven't been the most careful and I guess it's coming to bite me in the ass, but no. Absolutely not. It's not possible." She shook her head. "No way. There's just no time for a baby or for anything. It can't be happening."

"But you and Preacher haven't been careful."

"Okay, I will be honest here and admit I don't have the most … amazing relationship with men when it comes to wearing condoms. Oh, shit!" She covered her mouth. "I don't think I ever got tested when I came here. I'm going to have to talk to Randall about getting tested."

"I'm pretty sure they ran tests on you when you were in the hospital."

"But what if they didn't? What if they ... oh, my God. I can't think right now. This can't be happening to me." She sniffled. "I don't know if I'm ready."

"What about Bethany? You're doing wonderful with her."

"I ... I'm supposed to be meeting Preacher in a matter of hours."

Anne came to her, grabbing her hands. "Listen to me, you can cancel him. Just tell him whatever you need to for him to give you some space. Then we'll get a test on the way home and we'll see if it's even anything to worry about. It may be completely nothing, but there's no need to stress about anything, is there?"

"I don't ... I don't know."

"You don't have to worry about a thing." Anne stroked her hair back from her face. "Please, just try to relax."

"It's kind of hard to relax when I feel I'm spending every single waking moment freaking out."

"Take deep breaths. Long, deep breaths. It's fine. We don't know anything yet and we can make a decision as and when we do."

Robin nodded. She was calming down. She was fine. Nothing was going to go wrong.

****

"Are you avoiding me?" Preacher asked.

"No. No, of course I'm not avoiding you. We'll talk, I promise. I just don't feel so great right now."

"What about Bethany? Do you need me to come and look after her for you?"

Why was he being so sweet? She couldn't handle

this. She hadn't even told him about her suspicions, and he was offering to take care of her baby. He was ... everything. And she was a horrible person.

"No, it's fine. We'll talk tomorrow or when I'm feeling better, if that's okay."

"Yes. I'll be here waiting for you, always."

"Okay." She hung up the phone after saying goodbye, feeling awful.

"I put Bethany down for a nap after she ate. She's growing up so fast," Anne said. She held the small box within her grasp and seeing it made Robin feel a little woozy.

"I don't know if I can do this."

"You can do whatever the hell you want to do to." Anne sat down in the bedroom beside her bed. "There's no pressure here."

"It sure feels like it."

"Only because you're putting it on yourself." Anne placed the box down. "See, you don't have to take it. Nothing bad will happen. All you'll be doing is prolonging the answer, and believe me, that's no biggie."

Robin didn't make a move to pick it up. She kept debating with herself what she should or shouldn't do. To not take the test would mean she didn't have to worry about any of the answers. If she took the test, it would be a struggle to know and how to deal with it. She put a hand across her stomach, wondering what the hell to do.

"Why aren't you forcing me to take this test and to stop being a baby?" she asked.

"It's not my job to do this, Robin. I'm your friend. Your best friend, I don't want to force you to do anything." Anne sat there. "You know, when I took my first test, Elijah wasn't even there for me."

"He wasn't?"

"Nope. He made me take the test all on my own.

He told me to come over if it's a yes, and if I didn't turn up, he'd know we were in the clear." Anne laughed.

"You married this man?"

Anne snorted. "Yeah, I married him. I was young, stupid, and I really thought I was in love with him. We'd been together forever and well, I guess I thought he was the one. I'm such a loser, right?"

"You're not a loser. If I'm being totally honest, I thought Bishop would've been the guy I settled down with. There are times I wish we didn't lose our friendship, you know, but the more I think about it, it wasn't a real friendship. Bishop thought he owned me because of what was expected of us. You can't build anything on that, and when our friendship was tested, he pushed me away." She shrugged. "He failed epically."

"He's not the only friend you've got, Robin. Not anymore."

Robin sighed. "I need to know the answer. I need to know what to do."

"I'm here for you."

She picked up the box and disappeared into the bathroom. The last time she took one of these, her hands had been shaking so badly, just like they were now. Time or circumstance didn't seem to change this. Why couldn't men go through this? This was torture, and maybe men would learn the truth about how scary it was to face taking a test all on your own.

Taking a deep breath, she tried to focus, but it was so hard. Without looking at her reflection, she read through the instructions, complied with each one, and then stood waiting, gripping the edge of the sink as her future was decided.

Anne came in and took her hand as the stick showed them what she was going to have to do, and as it did, she felt a little sick to her stomach.

"It's going to be okay, Robin."

"You don't know that."

"I know Preacher is in love with you, and he will only ever see this as a good thing, and I think you should as well."

****

Sitting in the graveyard early in the morning wasn't exactly the best way to start a day. Robin sat on the cold, wooden bench. It was slightly damp from some rain the previous night, but she didn't care about the water, or the damp, or her clothes. Instead, she stared out at the graves. She read the ones closest to her, and she saw final resting places for moms, dads, aunts, sisters, so many people. So much life and of course, death.

Tears filled her eyes, and she didn't even know why she was here. There was no one for her to come and see. Her mother didn't get this luxury, nor did O'Klaren. She'd seen some of O'Klaren's family and they seemed to be doing a lot better without the man. He'd been a true monster. Beating his wife, hurting his kids. Sure, to the outside world, he'd painted a pretty picture but the very truth was one of misery.

Pain was something she was coming to know quite well.

"I have to say it's a shock to see you here."

She turned to see Bishop arriving. He sat down. No leather cut. Just a single jacket with no signals or ownership.

"I figured you'd have skipped town by now."

"Kind of can't. My dad warned me he'd put out an order to kill. It doesn't exactly inspire the traveling spirit."

She snorted. "I guess not." She looked out across to near the church. She'd never been inside. Never needed to pray or wanted to. Part of her had always assumed she'd be rejected for being Bear's daughter and her association with the Twisted Monsters MC. "How did we get here?"

"I walked here."

"I walked here too, but that wasn't what I meant."

"I know it wasn't but I was trying to be funny."

"Sorry, I'm not in a funny mood."

"I think we're both exactly where we need to be."

This made her turn toward him. They'd aged a little. They were no longer the carefree teens they'd once been.

"You think this was our life? How it was always supposed to be?"

"Obviously a lot of changes have been made, and I can't control the outcome of what happened, but we can't turn back the clock. We can't change what happened."

"When did you become all-knowing?" she asked.

"Right around the time my death was a real option." Bishop sighed. "You know, I never wanted you to be hurt or for anything bad to actually happen to you. It was never my intention for you to suffer."

"I did."

"I know, and I will never forgive myself for it. For a long time, even when you were with Reaper, I thought my actions were valid, you know? That I had some reason and pleasure at seeing Preacher not get what he wanted."

"Why do you hate your dad so much?"

"I don't. I was angry that he was able to get you when I couldn't get anything. I know you had feelings for him, and they grew so fucking fast."

"I loved you too."

"It's not the same."

"It could have been."

Bishop shook his head. "No, I messed that shit up when I started sleeping with random women and girls from school. I realize now my chance with you ended the moment Milly started her plan to hurt you. I wasn't there. I was more interested in what I could get. I wanted a woman dancing on my dick every second of every single day. You wouldn't even let me touch you, and I know when we did fool around, your heart was never in it. You were never there for me."

"I wanted to be."

"I know, but wanting to be and actually being there are two different things."

"You were my best friend."

"Exactly, I was your best friend and that's my fault. I realize that now. You never wanted to hurt me. Not even when you realized you were in love with my dad. You've always done whatever was needed to protect me and I've got to learn to walk on my own two feet. Don't get me wrong, I don't know exactly how long that's going to be. My dad isn't a man of many words, but I know he's a man of action."

"He won't kill you."

"You don't know that. I had hoped to make this right by finding Reaper, but that bastard turned up before I could even do that. I kept you guys in hiding, kept his location from Dad, and then, everything fucked up. I never meant for this, how it worked out. He'll kill me."

"He would have done it already."

"Wow, thank you for the vote of confidence. I was hoping he'd just forget I existed and I could go on my way and not look over my shoulder."

She smiled, but tears filled her eyes and she covered her face, hoping to hide the tears and gain control before they even got a chance to spill down, but she didn't have any such luck. She was broken, and right now, she needed a friend.

"Hey, hey. What is it?"

"You don't want to know."

"I do. I'm here now."

"No, you'll be angry and pissed, and I feel like we're sharing a moment."

"We've shared a lot of moments, but I'm here for you. You don't need to hide from me. I'm here and I'm not going to judge you. This is a judgment-free zone."

She sniffled. "I'm pregnant."

"Oh."

"Yeah. Are you going to get angry with me again?"

"Nope, but I think it's time you retake sex ed because you didn't pick up the clues about not getting pregnant. Condoms and all that."

"I don't need this right now," she said, also laughing along with him. "I do suck at this."

Bishop pulled her close and hugged her, kissing the top of her head. "I guess Preacher is the father?"

"Yes, which means you'll be a half-brother."

"If I survive."

"I don't see why you wouldn't."

"Robin, I was a traitor to the club. I fucked up and I failed in every single direction. We both know there's no right path for me anymore. I will face judgment by my dad and the club, and we know what happens to traitors."

"But you're still his son."

"I think I'm getting the hang of it, you know? I'm expecting death to come and when it does, I'll be ready for it." He nodded his head. "This is me being strong."

"Oh, Bishop, stop it." She patted his arm and laughed. It was good to finally laugh. It had been way too long. Why was her life constantly a mess?

"I do have to ask why you're sitting on a bench in a cemetery, staring out at a lot of graves, rather than going to tell my father the good news. We both know this will make him so happy."

"What if it doesn't?"

"I don't think it's possible for him to be miserable about this."

"What about Bethany? What about me? I'm a mess."

"You're not a mess, Robin. In fact, I think you're the perfect match to him in every single way. You don't take shit. You're a fighter, and if there's something I know about my father, he doesn't like weak people."

"What if I am weak?"

"Not possible." Bishop hugged her close. "I rented a car. I can drive you there. Where's Bethany?"

"Anne's watching her."

"Oh, right. Do you want that ride?"

"Yeah, I'd love it." What Bishop didn't know was that she still had a pocket knife on her. She had learned long ago the only way to protect herself was to always be armed in some way so no one could get the drop on her. If this was all fake and was Bishop's way of escaping town and using her as a tool to get what he wanted, he was going to be in for a fucking shock.

They drove together and she kept a close eye on the road and on Bishop. She wasn't going to let him get away with anything. Taking a deep breath, she waited.

Nothing.

He drove all the way to his father's without a single pitstop or even a hint of kidnapping.

Progress.

She thanked him for the ride and he smiled at her, wishing her good luck. She waited for him to pull out of the driveway before focusing on the house. She had always loved Preacher's house. It was private, peaceful, and seeing it now, she felt all the good memories. Yes, Reaper's taint was here as well, but overall, it wasn't everything. He would never win.

After walking up the steps, she came to a stop as Preacher opened the door. "Was that Bishop?" he asked.

"Yeah, he dropped me off. I hope that's okay." Why was she even asking? It was his son.

"He better not be leaving town."

"He's not, believe me. If anything, he's kind of waiting for your judgment. He knows if he leaves town, he's a dead guy." When did it become so easy to talk about things like this? It was completely and totally wrong.

Instead of saying anything more, she walked up the steps to face him. "We need to talk. Is now a good time or do you want me to leave?"

"It's always a good time with you." He stepped back and she had to brush past him, feeling the heat consume her body from the single touch.

This was why she could never leave, not now, not ever.

"Where's Bethany?" he asked.

"She's with Anne. I figured we could talk in private." She walked past the sitting room only to stop and turn back. Inside was a play den. "I don't recall … when did this happen?"

Girly toys filled the area. There was space to move around, but so many toys. It was a kid's dream.

"I wanted to make sure everything was ready for when you brought Bethany with you. I'm not pressuring you to move back in or anything, but I thought you should know I'm serious about you and about Bethany."

"Even though she's part Reaper?"

"She's part Reaper and all of you. I'm not going

to judge a kid based on their dad. Look at me. You know what I told you about my parents. I wouldn't do that."

He took her hands in his. "I know I'm probably not the right guy for the job. I fuck up more times than I can count, and I mess up everything. I love you. I want to be with you, and Bethany will be my daughter."

Tears filled her eyes. How could she not love this man? He was everything. Sweet, charming, loving, everything a woman could ask for.

"I'm pregnant," she said, letting the words slip out.

A MONSTER'S BEAUTY

Chapter Nine

"We've been here before," Randall said.

"We have." Robin sat on the table after the examination and blood was taken. "Am I healthy?"

"You are healthy. I do want to keep a close eye on you, just in case," he said. "You've been through a lot and I know Preacher will want to make sure you stay fit and healthy."

"Right." She stared down at the gown she'd been asked to put on. Preacher was outside waiting with Bethany. He hadn't come in this time. Why hadn't he come in? He'd taken the news of her pregnancy rather well. He'd been excited, lifting her up in his arms, kissing her and her stomach. Since he dropped her off at Anne's, though, on the very same day she'd told him a week ago, he'd been distant. This was the first time she'd seen him and that was to bring her to an appointment.

"You're not happy?" Randall asked.

"My emotions. I'm fine. Honestly. Just little things, they seem to be getting to me in ways I didn't realize they could. I'll be fine. I promise. It will all be good." She didn't know how long she could keep up the pretense. Even smiling was hurting her cheeks. The tears were constantly blurring her vision. "Actually, there is something I wanted to talk to you about. When I first arrived at the hospital. Something had happened to me and I was wondering if you tested me…" She stopped. It was so freaking hard for her to think or to feel right now.

"We took all the necessary bloodwork. You came back in the clear and healthy, Robin. You've got nothing to worry about."

She breathed out a sigh of relief. "That's good, right? It means this baby will be fine. No problems."

"You know I can't guarantee anything for you.

Babies, pregnancies, they all come with risks and problems. Some can be a breeze, like your first one. Then circumstances happen, and it all changes. I can't guarantee anything here, Robin. We can take it one day at a time and hope we catch anything of any concern."

"Right." She pressed her lips together.

"Then why do you look like you're going to throw up? You haven't experienced any morning sickness as yet, and you're doing fine. No problems."

"I'm fine."

"But?"

She stared at him, wondering what she should say to him. It was … impossible to not open up to him. "I don't think Preacher's happy." She whispered the words, not wanting to hear her fears.

Randall smiled. "That's not possible."

"He's not in here."

"He's taking care of Bethany, and on this first visit, I need to concentrate. Don't get me wrong, your little girl is a dream, but some kids can get restless and I need to be focused on you. Preacher knows that. He knows how important it is to take care of you. I promise you, he won't let anything happen to you. Not on his watch. Not on anyone's watch. You are the love of his life and I've known him a long time. It's a little shocking to even be saying those words."

"Love of his life?"

"In all the years I've known him, and I was there for your and Bishop's births. I held you both as newborn babies. Admittedly, I wasn't that much older than you."

She laughed because she knew he had to be because with him being a doctor, he'd completed far more training at her age. "I've never seen that man broken until the day you were gone. I know he nearly tore his club apart. He sacrificed a great deal to find you.

A MONSTER'S BEAUTY

He never did and each time it was a fail, he became more and more shattered. There was no way of consoling him. He loves you more than anything in the world and I truly believe if you were to say the club or you, he would pick you."

"Wow." She let the tears she'd been trying to keep at bay fall.

"Yeah, wow. I love my wife and kids, but I don't think I've ever experienced what you two do. The moment I called him, he was here to see you, Robin. The relief, even with your memory gone, he was just happy to have you back. There's more to Preacher than either of us will ever know, but his love for you, it will never be in question."

"Thank you."

"I'm going to let you get changed now. I've taken up enough of your time. Go and have some fun. You're going to need it." He left the room and as he did, she felt a little lighter, a little happier.

This hadn't sucked big time. There was a chance for her and for Preacher. She just had to stop letting her nerves and past experiences get in the way.

After changing into her clothes, she met Randall outside where he gave her a small birthing package that he'd given her with the first pregnancy. Leaflets, helplines, information, that kind of thing.

She met Preacher at the reception desk and she saw him paying. Bethany was in his arms and she was playing with his jacket, chewing on it.

She stepped up to him with a smile.

"All done?" he asked.

"Yeah, I'm all done."

She followed him outside to his waiting car. He put Bethany in her car seat and to stop her fussing, he handed her a little toy. "Is everything all good?"

"Yes. He can't give me any guarantees of a healthy baby, but what he can do is be supportive and be there." She lifted up her pack. "More stuff for me to read."

"I wanted to talk to you about moving back in with me. I know you want your own space, but I think now you should be around someone. I can drop you off at work. Bethany isn't ready for playschool yet but Anne assured me there's no problem with having her at work with you in the play area. I can pick you up. We can have lunch."

"Are you happy about the baby?" she asked.

Preacher jerked the car but quickly gained control. "Why the fuck would you think I wasn't happy about the baby? Is that why you've been silent with me and looked fucking miserable when I came to pick you up?" he asked.

She wanted to soothe him. To not make waves but at the same time, she was tired of being the one to constantly be the voice of reason. "I told you a week ago."

"Yeah, so?"

"Why haven't I seen you? I told you and I haven't seen you come near me. You haven't called or texted me. You haven't been by the library. You went completely silent on me and I don't understand it. I know a baby wasn't something we had planned."

"When have we ever planned it?"

"This isn't a time to joke around. I haven't had a very good relationship between the fathers of my children and my pregnancies and to be honest, I'm trying not to freak out right now. I know I unloaded this on you and it's a lot of pressure, but I'm dealing and I'm a lot younger than you."

Preacher pulled the car to a stop and she wanted

to storm out and walk away. It was what a child would do, but she didn't have that luxury.

"If you must know, a moment hasn't gone by when I haven't wanted to talk to you. To hear your voice, to know you're okay."

"All it would've taken was a single phone call."

"I know. I would've heard your voice and I would've come to you. You'll always be the person I come running to, Robin. I love you more than anything in the world and it scares me at times."

Tears filled her eyes at his honesty. She couldn't recall him ever being this open with her, only when she didn't have her memories, but that didn't completely count, did it?

"Since you told me about the pregnancy, I've had a lot of shit going down. I had some business to attend to with Dog. I've also gone to see my lawyer about your ability to marry. He's looking into your and Reaper's marriage."

"Oh." She didn't want to think about her marriage to Reaper. It had been something he'd forced her into and it didn't exactly contain many happy memories. Her life with Reaper confused her. Whenever she thought about him dead, she was a little sad. How could she not be? Bethany would grow up without a father. But then she would allow herself to remember the first couple of weeks he'd taken her. The horror, the pain, the abuse. She'd suffered it all at his hands, and he hadn't cared. He'd laughed because as far as he was concerned, he'd been hurting Preacher through her.

Reaper's entire plan had been to get her pregnant and make her love him. She had loved him in a way, but not completely, and certainly not after knowing what he'd done. Those men had hurt her in ways she didn't like to think about. Those memories were the ones she no longer wanted or needed.

"I'm not angry at you about what happened. I love you more than anything in the world. I would die for you."

"You don't have to be so drastic," she said, trying to smile.

Whenever he told her that he loved her, it always, without fail, brought happiness into her heart. There were no other words for it. "I don't think I could live with anything happening to you."

"Nothing will happen to me."

"You're so sure of yourself."

"I know my limits. I know what I need to do."

"I sometimes worry that he's not gone," she said. The words were a mere whisper as she was too afraid to say them out loud.

"He is."

"How do you know?"

"Robin, I'm not going to go into the details, but by the time I was finished with him, they would never have been able to identify him. That's how good I was."

"Oh."

"Yeah, oh."

She looked down at his hands. They were a lot larger than hers but they provided her with so much love and comfort. "I can't lose this, not again."

"You won't."

"I'm scared, Preacher."

He gripped the back of her neck, pulling her close. "You've got nothing to be afraid of. There's no way I'd let anyone hurt you. You've got to believe that."

"I do. I just … what if something bad happens with the baby? What if someone tries to take it from us again? I know what it's like to go through that pain. I don't think I can stand it again. What if we're cursed? If we can never have kids of our own?"

"You're worried about a lot," he said. "We're not cursed. I don't believe in curses. The last time we were pregnant, I didn't deal with O'Klaren swiftly enough. The death of our child is on my shoulders."

She shook her head. "No. I don't believe that. I can't. No, I won't let you think you're responsible like that."

He took her hand, locking their fingers together, and smiled. "If I'd dealt with him, we wouldn't be having this conversation. Bethany wouldn't have been born and we'd have been together."

She allowed herself a few minutes to merely think about what their life could have been like if nothing had gone wrong. "We'd have been happy."

"And we're always going to be happy."

"I was scared with Bethany as well," Robin said. "There were a couple of complications along the way, but I think I was the one with the problem. I was always so afraid."

"You've got nothing to be afraid of anymore. You've got me, the club, and I'm not letting anything happen to you. I've got all my bases covered. Now, do you think we can go home so I can put Bethany down for a nap and make you some food?"

"I'd love that."

"Good." He cupped her cheek, leaning forward and kissing her. It wasn't a possessive kiss. "Now, stop worrying. I won't let you worry about shit like this. We're going to get through it together. Like always."

****

Preacher paced up and down the long floor as Dog and his men counted out the night's quota of money. It had been a blood bath, one Preacher had been too distracted to enjoy.

"Not that I don't enjoy our little chats and coming together as a family, but is there a reason you're rubbing out the floor?" Dog asked.

"You ever had a kid?"

Dog's laughter echoed around the warehouse. "You're joking, right?"

"I'm not joking. If I was joking, I wouldn't be staring at you, wondering what the fuck was going on." He didn't like being laughed at.

"Let's go and talk about this." Dog took the lead, heading upstairs to one of the balconies overlooking the main fighting ring. Not much of a ring. Just the floor marked with some chalk. If either man ended up outside of the chalk, they were killed. The stricter the rules, the hungrier the crowd got for someone to slip up.

Dog pulled out a pack of cigarettes, lit one, and handed it to him. "You need this."

"Robin's pregnant."

"So I heard."

"How the fuck do you hear?"

"A visit to Randall, people talk."

"My men better not fucking talk."

"I've got guys who can hack into any kind of shit for the right price. I wanted to know what was going on, so I got everything checked out. How is she?"

"She's ... fuck, I don't know how she is." Preacher ran a hand down his face. In order to deal with business, he'd dropped her back off at Anne's to stay. He'd offered to pay the woman, but she'd glared at him and told him the next time he offered to pay her, she'd kick him in the balls for his disrespect. She'd slammed the door on his face and within seconds, opened it and apologized, saying she wouldn't hurt him at all. She didn't believe in violence.

"Your woman's knocked up and you don't know

how she's doing. What kind of fucking saint are you?"

"I'm not a saint."

Dog snorted, taking a deep inhale on his cigarette before blowing it out, pluming smoke traveling up until it dissipated. "When it comes to your woman, you're a saint. I've never known a guy who nearly gave up everything to find this one woman. It made me wonder so many times if this chick has a magnet for a pussy, or a super one. I don't know."

"Watch it."

"What? A guy's got to know what makes another guy go crazy, right?"

"I'm not crazy."

"Dude, did you even look in the mirror when you went all over trying to find ghosts? That's what you did." Dog laughed. "People thought it made you look weak and shit."

"You didn't?"

"No, hell, no, I thought it made you look a little more interesting." Dog stopped to take another long drag on his cigarette. "Now, don't get me wrong. I don't understand the feelings and I didn't see whatever magic she's got going on when I came for dinner, but shit, Preacher, you were pacing, waiting for money. What gives?"

Preacher stared at him, and Dog held his hands up.

"We can pretend we're not friends for a little longer, if you'd like. We both know the truth."

"We're not friends. We're business associates."

Dog snorted. "Right. Like you wouldn't give a shit if you ever found out one of my boys was planning to off me. It happened just last week, in case you were wondering."

"Wait? What?"

"Yeah, the fuck, right? I can't believe it myself. Who the fuck can buy loyalty these days? I know I can't. I treat my boys well, you know. Give them a good life. Give them a good fucking reason for living and what do I get? Fuck all. That's what I get." He shook his head. "It's all bullshit."

"What happened?"

"To cut a long story a little short, one of my boys didn't like taking orders from me anymore, and so in his way to deal with it, he made a deal to deliver my severed head."

Preacher looked down at his neck.

"You won't find it severed. I stopped him before he could even get close. I look like a pretty boy, but believe me, my muscles can make a man hurt in ways they don't even realize. It's all good, though. This is the kind of shit I live for."

He took a deep breath. "He wanted the money. The power, and I guess he wanted to have the reputation for taking me out."

"It wasn't my boy, was it?" Preacher asked, chuckling. He had to go and deal with Bishop one day.

"Nope. Your boy comes anywhere near my camp, I'm sending his ass straight back to you. The kid thinks he's all big and tough but he won't last five minutes in a ring like this. Without realizing it, he likes rules. It's why he pretty much broke apart over all the Reaper bullshit."

"There really is a brain inside that head of yours, isn't there?"

"I've told you before, I'm a hell of a lot more than a pretty fucking face," Dog said, giving him a little pout.

"Yeah, I'm not going to date you anytime soon." Preacher finished his cigarette, staring down at the ring. "You know, I've never known real fear. I always thought fear was for pussies. There's nothing to be afraid of when you're the biggest, baddest motherfucker around. I've never had anything to lose. Whatever I've wanted, I've taken, and anything I don't want, I don't even bother to fucking hunt for."

"Why are we getting all, you know, touchy-feely?"

"You want to be my friend. Friends listen."

"Since the fuck when?"

"Since forever. You want to be BFFs, this is what a BFF does. We listen to each other."

"Can I change the dynamic of our friendship?"

"You could be my bitch." Preacher laughed. "Fuck, what have we become?"

"I've worn you down. So, you've never felt fear?" Dog lit a new cigarette.

"No, not until recently, have you?"

"Yes, all the fucking time," Dog said. He pointed at his face. "Let's face it, I didn't have an easy childhood. Where other kids were asking Santa for toys and shit, I was begging to be found, to find someone who would care about me and not hurt me. If you ever tell another living soul, I will fucking gut you, got it?"

"I'd like to see you try, but if you think I'd admit to anyone I got all touchy-feely for you, I'd deny it."

"So we're both good on denying everything. Good to know. I've known fear as a boy. I can't walk away from who I was or what I've become. I used to think fear made me weak, but it doesn't. Fear pushes us. It drives us. It makes us the men we are and it makes us strong."

Dog pointed down at his men. "All of them can tell you a story. Some worse than mine, some better. All of them are monsters and have been created because of circumstances. It's never going to change who they are.

They are what we've been made. Fear makes us. It forces us to make decisions we didn't know we were even capable of making."

"I'm scared I'm not going to be able to protect her," he said.

"Do you have another enemy lurking in the shadows?"

"No. I have plenty of enemies. Most of them are dead." Preacher ran a hand down his face. "She's afraid."

"Then be there for her. Don't be talking to me about shit when the true person you should be talking to is your woman. Robin, she wants you right now, I'm guessing."

"I feel my life is really fucked up when I'm taking advice from you."

"I give great advice. You should take it. I do know what I'm talking about."

"It's counted," one of the men down below said, yelling up to be heard.

"Good."

"It's time for us to split."

"If you ever need backup, or to deal with your boys, let me know."

"Will do, but one thing I can promise you, fear or not, I know how to take care of myself." They made their way downstairs. Preacher took their cut and made their way outside to find Bear staring up at the sun.

"What do you think about women staying with cheating assholes?" Bear asked as he moved closer.

"Are we talking about Rebecca?" Preacher asked.

"No. Why the fuck would you think that?"

"You were a cheating asshole."

"No, I'm talking about Anne."

"Anne? Robin's Anne?"

"Who else would I be talking about?"

"I don't know. I figured you'd expanded your friendship base? For all I know, you could have been reading about an Anne in a book."

"Cut the shit, Preach. What do you think about it?"

"One, I don't think about it. Two, she's Robin's friend. Three, I'm guessing it's because of the kids."

"Do you think she'll care if I kill him?"

"Do you think a woman would care if you killed the man who fathered their kids?" Preacher didn't like the bitterness. "Well, I killed Reaper, and me and Robin are doing well. I'm sure Anne would feel the same."

"You think I don't know when I can detect sarcasm?"

"I don't know what you think you can detect half of the time. If you try to kill Elijah—that's the husband's name—you're heading to fail. Now, I've got to go and see my woman." He straddled his bike and paused. "Are you and Anne ... together?"

"No, we're not together. I'm just curious."

"Do you like her?"

"I ... no, we're just friends. I have to make sure my daughter is being cared for."

"But I'm the one doing that, so tell me again, what exactly is it you're doing."

"None of your business."

"Oh, but it is my business if you're going to hurt my woman."

"Look, I like Anne. Nothing has happened and she won't leave Elijah. Let's just leave it alone. I'm not getting into this all again." Bear straddled his own bike. "How is Robin?"

"Why don't you ask her yourself?" He was getting tired of being Bear's confidant when it came to his daughter. If he wanted to know what Robin was going through, he should go and see her.

Like him, he should go tell her the truth.

"I'll see her when I'm ready."

He was bored with the conversation and so he gunned the engine and started to take off.

"You know you're going to kill me. I can see the look in your eyes, but you're going to have to know you will never really be rid of me. I've been a part of Robin. She's part of me. Bethany will always be there unless you kill a harmless little baby. Do you think you can do that?"

Reaper's words threatened to haunt him.

It wasn't his memory he had a problem with. He could deal with whatever pain and destruction the bastard did. It wasn't hard to do. The man hadn't been a saint to anyone. Robin was better off without him, and in the past couple of days, since learning the truth of her pregnancy, he'd seen her so happy. There were moments when fear got the better of her. He'd watch her holding her stomach, whispering, almost as if she was begging for something not to go wrong. He hated those days more than anything else.

He had no words to help her believe everything was going to be okay. She only knew the pain of loss, and there was nothing he could do about it.

Riding back to town, he made his first stop at the clubhouse in order to deal with the profits from the latest fight. It was a huge sum of money and a percentage always went into the club safe, to help with any emergencies in case their banks were frozen or their homes raided.

It had happened to a couple of the guys, and Preacher liked to prepare for everything. No matter how big or how small it might be. Once he'd done his job for the club, he got back on his bike and rode toward Anne's house. Not that it was much of a surprise for Bear to follow him.

When they arrived at Anne's house, Preacher noticed the husband's family car and glanced back at Bear, who was also looking at it.

This wasn't his problem. Whatever went down between Anne and Bear, it was between them and he wouldn't allow himself or his woman to get caught up in the crossfire.

Elijah opened the door. His cheeks tensed as his teeth clenched.

"I'm here to see Robin."

"My home is not a hotel."

"Good." He pushed past him. "Because I'm not paying."

"Preacher, it's good to see you," Anne said. She held a glass of wine in hand. "Bethany is asleep, and Robin's curled up on the sofa." She pointed into the room and he followed her direction to see his woman. She was curled up and looked so damn cute. "She's been fine all night. We watched a couple of movies. I had the wine, she had the hot chocolate. It's all been good."

Elijah cleared his throat. "Are we having to give a room for two of them now?"

Anne's cheeks heated as she looked at Bear.

There was something going on there but it wasn't his business. "Can I have a few minutes alone with her?"

"Of course. Come on." Anne took charge, herding the other men out of the way.

"Are you fucking kidding me right now? This is my house and you're letting him just go walk about."

"Shut up, Elijah."

Preacher drowned them out, stepping into the room. For a few seconds, he simply watched her. One of her hands was curled up beneath her head and the other covered over her stomach, trying to protect herself and their baby.

Sitting down beside her, he pulled her into his arms and as he did so, she woke up.

"Preacher?" There was a slight panic to her tone, but he calmed her down.

"Yeah, it's just me."

"Business didn't take as long as you thought it would?"

"No, it didn't."

She snuggled in close. "I've missed you."

"I missed you too, baby." He kissed the top of her head. "How long has Elijah been here?"

"He's been grumbling all afternoon. Anne thinks his latest conquest dumped his ass."

"It would serve him right."

"Yeah, it would. I don't think she's happy when he constantly comes by. I think it bothers her."

"Do you want me to take care of it?"

"No. If she wants it taken care of, she'll ask you. This is nice." She breathed in his scent. "You smell nice."

He laughed. "I've been driving and smoking."

"I guess I've missed you a lot."

"Robin, I'm so sorry," he said.

She lifted her head. "Why? What's wrong?"

"I've tried to put a brave face on everything but I can't do it anymore. I love you more than anything in the world. You know that, right?"

"Yes."

"I don't want anything to happen to you. I love you so damn much. You mean the world to me and I want us to have this baby." He covered her hand with his.

"It scares me as well. I sometimes worry Randall got it wrong and I won't be able to ever have our baby."

A MONSTER'S BEAUTY

She sniffled and he wiped the tears from beneath her eyes.

"I won't hide my fears from you anymore. I'll give you whatever you need and we will take this one day at a time."

"I do love you, Preacher."

He took possession of her mouth. It wasn't easy admitting fear, and it wasn't the true extent of his feelings either, but it was a start and right now, it was more than he could ask for.

****

"I don't like having them in my house," Elijah said.

Bear snorted.

Anne looked at her husband. "It's my house as well, and they're friends."

"Since when did you become friends with a bunch of bikers?"

"Around the time I finally accepted you couldn't keep your dick in your pants. We both have something that happens that we don't like. So deal with it. I have to." She finished off her wine glass. "Now I'm not going to keep on fighting about all of this. If you're not happy with my friends, divorce me."

"What?"

"I know we said we'd keep everything together for the kids and I still want to try that, but I'm not going to keep putting my happiness on hold just because you can't stand the kinds of people I'm friends with. I have to put up with the gossip behind my back. All you've got to do is deal with the people I make friends with. No one gossips about me. Deal with it, or divorce me. I need some air."

Anne stepped outside, pulling her robe around her. She took several deep breaths, trying to feel calm.

This couldn't be happening. She thought she could stay with Elijah and make all of this work, but each time he was near her, she kept finding it harder to even put up with him.

Was she being strong keeping her family together for the sake of her kids? Or lazy? Or complacent? Should she divorce him, deal with her upset kids, and find some happiness for herself?

The door opened and she turned to see Bear coming closer.

"How are you?" he asked.

"I'm fine. Or I will be when I know what the hell I'm doing. Nothing makes any sense to me anymore. I'm trying to keep it all together but at every single turn, I seem to always be failing. I don't know what I'm doing anymore."

Bear grabbed her shoulders and held her tightly. She shouldn't be having feelings for this man, but as he pulled her back, she couldn't not want him. It was wrong. He was at her house, and she had to show some respect at least.

"I can't do this."

"We're not doing anything wrong."

"No, you're not doing anything wrong, but I am. I've got to get my shit together. I'm sorry, I can't do this. I'm so sorry."

Anne walked away and as she did, she couldn't help but feel she was leaving part of her soul behind.

A MONSTER'S BEAUTY

Chapter Ten

"I shouldn't be surprised I'd find you here. I mean, after all, a *no* really doesn't mean no to a guy like you, does it?" Principal Arnold said.

Preacher lifted his feet and placed them right on top of the man's desk. "I don't know. It depends on if you set me certain boundaries." He smirked as Arnold looked angry. "Now I tried to do this amicably, but you've gone and made it all a little personal, which is more than fine, believe me. I can handle whatever bullshit you throw at me. It's not a problem, but you're hurting Robin."

"No, what I'm doing is simply saying she can't come and have the best kind of education your dirty money can buy. Robin failed to graduate, and well, we all know what happens to women who fail at school. She has become just another impressive statistic."

Preacher sighed. He stared at the man opposite him and ran his tongue across his teeth. This was pissing him off. It fucking annoyed him. Arnold was a piece of work. The world judged him because he wore his true colors on his leather cut. This was who he was and he wasn't ashamed of the world knowing him, of seeing him, of all of it.

"You know, I'm growing tired of all of this bullshit." He slid his boot across the desk, sending all of the contents spilling to the floor. He released a breath. "Ah, that feels so much better."

He did the same with the other foot until the desk was empty, at which point he got to his feet.

"You're going to let Robin back in and do you know why I know you're going to let her back in?"

"Because you're going to torture me if I don't?"

"There is that, and I've got to say I do love the

sound of that, but it's not the only reason. No, you're going to let her in because if you don't, I will make sure this is front-page news."

He held up his cell phone. He didn't know how Cheeky got so close without either Arnold or his latest schoolgirl obsession realizing it.

In the photo, Arnold was very much naked behind the driver's seat of the car, his hands all over the girl.

"I've got to say, do you think she's eighteen? Did you know it's an offense to be with a minor?" It was a little hypocritical of him to judge, but he didn't prey on schoolgirls, and he happened to know Arnold liked to leave a long line of them. "Now, do you want this to be made public? I can make it happen. It would be so easy."

"What exactly do you want?"

"I want you to open up your teaching staff where Robin needs the extra help, and I want her to be able to graduate within the next year. She didn't get the chance to and I want her to have what her heart desires."

"And if I refuse?"

"I'm not a very nice person when I don't get what I want. By all means, we can have this fight, but you're not going to win." Preacher perched on the edge of the desk.

"How do I know you won't send that out?"

"Regardless of what you think, a deal's a deal. You're not hurting this girl and it looks to me like she's very happy to be with you." Preacher shrugged. "I can't accuse the girl of bad taste. I can, but I won't. So how about we settle this? Are you going to give me what I want, or will I be pressing this magic button?"

Arnold glared at the phone. "If she doesn't attend one of the classes—"

"You'll do what? Don't think you've got the power to negotiate here. I've got all the power. All you have to do is help her. That's all I ask."

"Fine. She can start tomorrow."

"No, today. I want to give her a special treat and the only way I do that is by making sure she has all the paperwork today. I've got all day. Come on, get it done."

With every passing second, Preacher found torturing him so much fun. He held all the power and people like Arnold believed they were better than men like him. Like he had some kind of ulterior motive, but it was all bullshit. Arnold was just as bad as him, if not worse. There was no difference between them. He sat in Arnold's office as each teacher Robin would need supplied him with the necessary paperwork. It was fun to get under his skin. It really made for a lot of fun. Fun he hadn't been expecting, but it was there regardless.

When he had everything he needed, it was lunchtime, and so he left the high school, feeling happy. On his way back into town, he came to a stop when he caught sight of Bishop. He was carrying out a large bag of what looked like bird feed. He placed in the back of an old man's pickup, wiping his hands before he caught sight of him.

"Hey, Dad," Bishop said.

"So I'm *Dad* now."

"To be honest, I don't know what to call you. It's not like I've got some kind of knowledge about what's happening to me." Bishop shrugged. "Did you make a decision?"

Preacher wasn't going to pretend he didn't know what his son was talking about. "No. I haven't really thought about you or what I should do with you."

"Ouch. I'm surprised the boys haven't ordered you to deal with my ass long before now."

"You think I don't know you helped us to locate the Slaves to the Beast? Without your help, I wouldn't have been able to take them out."

"Yeah, well, if it wasn't for me, I wouldn't be out in the cold like this, and I'd still have Robin. She never would've been taken and I wouldn't be one of the world's biggest fuck-ups, but I can't go back and change what I did."

"You think of yourself as a fuck-up?"

"Aren't I?"

"I honestly don't know anymore." Preacher didn't have it in him to get into this argument with his son. There was nothing he could do to change the past. No way of stopping what was to come. "You're working here now?"

"Yeah, it's a good way to make a living."

"It is? Hauling birdseed?"

"It beats sitting at home all day waiting for the bullet."

"When your time comes, you'll know about it." Preacher looked around and he caught several people watching them. "Did you hear about Robin?"

"I heard. Congratulations?"

"You're not pissed?" Preacher asked.

"Nah, I lost the right to be anything a long time ago. I'm happy for the two of you. I'm pleased you were able to work your shit out in your own way. It's what is supposed to happen. I wish you both a lot of success this time."

Someone called his name. "I've got to go."

Preacher didn't stop him from leaving. It was the best thing for him to do. Rubbing the back of his head, he tried to think of something to say but came up with nothing. The only reason the guys hadn't been hassling him about taking care of Bishop was purely down to his help in eliminating the whole of Slaves to the Beast.

Running a hand across his face, he continued his

way toward the library where Robin was working. Anne had taken the day off and was taking care of Bethany. Entering the library, he saw her standing at the desk, clicking away on the computer. For a few seconds, he simply watched her.

Before she was taken from him, he'd never gotten the luxury of being able to watch her. Right now, she looked so lost in thought, like nothing was bothering her. She was busy working, her fingers dancing over the keys. He'd taken her for granted, he knew that now, but he also knew he would never allow his own fears or the club to come between them.

He stepped toward the desk. "Hello, beautiful. I'm not looking for a book but the love of a woman."

She chuckled. "Hello." She put her hands on the counter and leaned across, kissing his lips. "I've missed you."

"It's only been a couple of hours since you last saw me."

"And already it feels like too long. Not that I don't mind you being here, but it's rare to see you inside the library." She tucked some of her hair behind her ear. She'd removed the blonde dye Reaper had forced her to wear, and those gorgeous brown locks he loved so much were in pride of place. He would never get her to change. He didn't need her to.

"I want to invite you to dinner tonight."

"You'll be cooking dinner?"

"Like always."

"Then I don't need an invite." She giggled. "You're being silly."

"Can you call Anne? Ask her to keep an eye on Bethany for us?"

"Of course. I don't think she'll mind. Do you want to tell me what all of this is about?"

"Not really." He gripped the back of her neck. "Don't get into any trouble now."

"I won't."

He left her alone and headed instead to Billy at the police station.

Billy was at the front desk, once again, and someone else was typing away at a computer. "You know those things are going to kill you one day."

"You're a computerphobe."

"I don't like things I don't understand. This little machine has way too much information on it and at the same time, not enough."

"This isn't a social call?" Billy asked.

"It's a whatever-you-want-to-call-it call so I can get what I want."

"Edward Myers was in touch yesterday. He gave me the details of the man who performed the ceremony for Reaper and Robin. It turns out he wasn't ordained or in any way capable of creating a binding and legal marriage. Now, Robin and Bishop's marriage was annulled and done through the proper channels."

"So Robin's free to marry?"

"She can marry whoever she wants to. You don't think you're moving a little fast, though?"

"Why do you think I'm going to ask her?" Preacher asked.

"You're finding out all of this information and it's got to be for a reason, right? I'm not stupid. You're finally going to ask Robin to marry you."

"This is none of your business."

"This is a big freaking deal."

"Billy, I like you. We've gotten along together for some time now. You've always had my back, but I'm telling you to back the fuck off. Now do you have the paperwork to state Robin isn't married?"

Billy held up the file. "Free of charge, and I better get an invite to the wedding."

Preacher took the file and left. After he made a quick stop at the club to catch up with his boys on some of the goings-on around the club, he tried not to think about what he had planned for the night.

He had already talked to Bear and he'd given him the all-clear to ask for his daughter's hand in marriage, but it didn't make it any easier. In fact, it only seemed to make it a little harder.

Running fingers through his hair, he tried not to be nervous.

What the fuck did he have to be nervous about?

He was the president of the Twisted Monsters MC. He gave monsters a reason to fear.

Robin was his light. She was his reason for breathing, for being anything.

"I'm totally and royally fucked."

With all the necessary bills dealt with, and Dog already organizing the next fight, he closed up his office, locked it, and headed out. He made a quick stop at the local grocery store. People were back to giving him a wide berth, which he had no problem with. One of the downsides to Robin's kidnapping, people were more than willing to come and share their sympathy with him as if she was actually dead. His woman wasn't dead, and she hadn't been.

With a bunch of ingredients, he got home and started to make her a delicious meal. One of her favorites was his stir-fry, and he wanted to impress her. With everything ready, he waited for Bear to bring her home.

At the sound of his friend's car, he went to the door and watched as Robin kissed her father on the cheek and ran up the stairs to him. She threw herself into his arms. "Anne had no problem looking after Bethany but she did tell me to tell you to make me scream." Robin's face was bright red. "I think whoever she's seeing is having a very big influence on her."

"You think she's dating?"

"I think something is going on there. I've seen a difference in her and I recognize the signs. I even heard her tell Elijah to go fuck off and screw another of his skanks."

"And that's not normal?"

"Not for Anne. Don't get me wrong, if her kids aren't around, she can curse like anyone, but even when they're not, she kind of keeps control of herself. It makes more sense when you get to know her, I promise."

"She's your friend."

"That she is. So what's so important about tonight?"

He pulled her into his home. "First, I want you to relax."

"Done. Easy to do and done."

"Good." He led her through to his dining room and poured her a glass of water with ice.

"Preacher, this is … is this a date? I didn't dress for a dinner date."

"Don't worry and don't stress. This is all on me. I promise. Now, I want you to relax while I go prepare your food."

"You're slaving for me?"

"I'm cooking for you." He took her hand, kissing the knuckles. "I'll be right back."

He went straight to the kitchen and started to work on their meal. All it took was fifteen minutes as he'd done all of the chopping before she arrived. This was another reason he loved stir-fry. It was so easy and fast to do.

Food served, he took her a bowl. "Dig in."

"Food, water, candlelight. I think you're trying to seduce me."

"Is it working?"

"A little."

"I wanted to talk to you about something. A couple of things, actually." He took another scoop of noodles before grabbing the file he'd glanced over with Billy. "Take a look."

"I don't have a clue what I'm looking at."

"You and Reaper were never married. We don't have to wait for him to be declared dead before I can marry you," he said.

"Wait? What? No, there was a ceremony."

"The man he used didn't have the power to marry you. He couldn't do the service. It was all fake."

"All this time we weren't married?"

"No."

"Oh."

"Are you sad about that?" he asked.

"What? Oh, no, I'm not sad."

Preacher didn't believe her. "Then why do you look like I've just given you some of the worst news you could have possibly gotten?"

"I'm sorry. It's not that. I can't believe this is all. I know it's the truth, but I guess I was kind of … I don't know."

"You thought you were married."

"Yeah. I don't miss him. My memories with Reaper will always be messed up. You understand that, right?"

"I do." He also didn't like it and doubted he ever would. Reaper had fucked with his woman's head, and if he could go back, he would totally kill him all over again, only this time, he'd go slow, really fucking slow. "I know this is a lot to take in and I don't expect an answer now. I want you to think about it." He pulled out the engagement ring he'd spent hours looking for. It was only a small diamond. Small but beautiful. His love for Robin was the one good part of him.

She owned him in ways he didn't even believe she realized, but he belonged to her. He'd give her whatever she asked for, no questions asked.

"Will you marry me?" He pressed his fingers to her lips. "No answers. I've given you a lot to think about already and I know I'm a bit of a bastard for doing it. No answers. I won't even take your answer now. You've got to hold on to it until I'm ready to hear it."

"Okay."

"I've got something else."

"Preacher, I don't know how much more I can take."

"This isn't bad, I promise. It's not bad." He got to his feet, grabbing the paperwork he'd gotten and placed it in front of her. "If you still want to graduate, then I got all of your teachers on board. They're willing to help you get what you need in order to graduate either at the end of this year, before, or when you need to."

Robin's hand shook as she touched the top of the file. "You … how? I know Arnold hates me. He's still the principal of the school. There's no way he would've even let me back in."

"He didn't need to have a reason, Robin. I asked and we came to an arrangement."

"You blackmailed him?"

"Blackmail is such an ugly word, is it not?"

"You did, didn't you?"

Preacher smiled. "Let's just say he knows it's in his best interest if he wants to keep his life in order."

"I'm shocked and speechless. I don't have a clue what to say." She released a breath. "Thank you so much.

A MONSTER'S BEAUTY

I've been wanting to graduate for so long."

"I know, and now is your chance. All you've got to do is put in the hard work."

"What about Bethany? My job?"

"Robin, I'm going to take care of you. You don't need to worry about any of those things. Between myself, Anne, and Bear, we'll get this done."

"Wow, I have an answer for you."

"Not now. I don't want to hear it."

"When do you want to hear it?"

"When I'm ready and I'll ask for it." He kissed her lips, silencing any more questions.

****

Robin wasn't married.

She could marry whomever she wanted.

There was no boundary on her. Nothing holding her back. Apart from Preacher, who didn't want to know her answer. She kissed him back, feeling an awakening within her body. She wanted his hands, his mouth, his everything all over her. To feel him surround her.

"Take me to bed," she said.

He lifted her into his arms and he didn't give anything away about her being too heavy. Preacher carried her upstairs to his bedroom. He placed her on the floor, and she put her hands on his chest, feeling the rush of his heartbeat.

"Do you have any idea what it is you do to me?" he asked.

"I imagine it's the same as what you do to me." She slid her hand down, reaching between his thighs to cup his dick. "I can feel how much you want me."

"Are you willing to show me how much you want me?" he asked, his palm rubbing against her pussy.

She gasped as he rubbed. The fabric of her jeans slid over her sensitive pussy. She couldn't get enough of his touch.

She begged for more and he gave it to her. Nibbling on her lip, she gasped, hungry, desperate, aching, wanting, and needy.

He let go of her pussy and his hands went to her shirt. He wasn't gentle as he grabbed the edges of her shirt, tugging it open, and the buttons sprang across the room.

She moaned his name as his lips took possession of one nipple. His tongue slid across the peak. Back and forth he flicked and she watched him.

He cupped both of her tits, pressing them together. "I can't get enough of these fat, juicy tits. So big."

"Please."

"You want me to stop?"

"No, don't ever fucking stop."

"I like it when you talk dirty."

"Please."

"You want me to lick on these sweet tits?"

"Yes."

"Do you want me to do a lot more?"

"Yes."

"Tell me what you want," he said.

Robin moaned. She didn't know if she had the ability to tell him what she wanted. He continued to tease her tits, tonguing each hard peak, and she melted. "I want you to…"

"Yeah, baby, tell me what you want," he said.

"I don't think I can."

He stopped licking at her tits. He stared at her, holding her breasts. "If you can't tell me then I guess I should stop."

"No!" She growled. "You know I'm not good at this."

A MONSTER'S BEAUTY

"Then do me a favor," he said. "Try."

"I don't think I can."

He sighed. He dropped her tits but she didn't have to wait long. His fingers ran down her back, sliding up into her hair. "Do you want to know what I want to do to you?" he asked.

"No." She had an idea, but she wanted to hear him say the words. Why couldn't she be open and honest with him? He'd given her so much already. They had finally found each other and she didn't want to lose him, or any part of him.

"Then I better tell you. I want to keep sucking on these tits because they are so incredibly big. I can't wait until they're full and ripe." He teased over one nipple as he stroked the other, using the inner palm of his hand and his thumb and finger to tweak. He let go of her tits and slid his hand down, stroking to her navel before dancing across the band of her jeans. He fingered the lining and she gasped, not wanting him to stop.

"Then I'm going to strip off these jeans. I want you naked, spread open, and begging for my dick. You're going to look so pretty. I bet I'll make your cunt wet and ready for me. I'm going to make you come with my mouth, and I'm going to fill and stretch you with my fingers. When I put my dick in you, I want to slide in so easily because there's nothing in my way to stop me."

"Please," she said, with a whimper.

"I'm going to watch your pretty pussy open for me, sucking my dick in like it's supposed to. Your tits are going to bounce and I'm going to grab your hips, and I'm going to make you come again before I even think of finding my own release. By the time I'm done with you tonight, Robin, every single time you move, you're going to remember this moment and you're going to love me even more for it. Now do you think you can speak as dirty as that?"

Robin didn't know how dirty she could go, but seeing the excitement in Preacher's eyes, she knew she wanted to give it a try. "I want you to keep on playing with my tits. I love it when you suck on them." She licked her lips as she didn't know what else to say to him but what she wanted.

"You want it like this?" he asked. His tongue flicked across her nipple. Then he used his teeth, creating enough pain that he then soothed back out again. Each touch sent more and more pleasure rushing through her body.

"Yes."

"Tell me more."

"I love it when you put your tongue on my…" She didn't know if she could say it or not. It seemed so dirty and wrong, but she wanted to. She couldn't get enough of him. "Please, Preacher."

"Tell me."

"I want you to lick my pussy. I love it when you tease and play with me. I can't get enough of it and it makes me want it even more."

"That's right, baby, I'm going to lick this pretty pussy." He moved her toward the edge of the bed, sitting her down and pushing her back. Her stomach wasn't showing her pregnancy just yet but by the time he was done with her, she was going to be swollen with his kid.

As he ran his fingers all over her stomach, she watched him while he looked at her with awe.

"I never want you to stop touching me like that," she said.

"I won't. I promise. Spread those pretty thighs for me."

She opened her legs and he groaned. "A man could get used to this," he said.

"I hope you never stop wanting me."

"It's not going to be a problem." With her legs spread, he breathed her in, and she watched, not wanting to look away from the way he kept watching her. She wanted to belong to him in every single way that counted.

When his tongue teased across her slit, she cried out, hungry for more. He grabbed her ass, holding her up to his mouth as he licked and ravished her pussy. Each taste drove her closer to the edge of bliss, wanting to completely fall off.

"Do you have any idea how fucking hot you make me?" he said.

"Please."

"You want to come all over my face?"

"Yes."

"Good." He licked and sucked at her clit, bit down on the swollen nub. Making her scream and beg for more until she couldn't take it anymore and her release rushed over her, sending her over the edge and into a pleasure unlike anything she'd ever felt before in her life. She screamed his name, not wanting him to stop but unable to take the pleasure that was attacking her from his mouth.

"I'm going to make sure you feel every single part of me." He nibbled on her thigh and moved her up the bed until she was resting against the pillows. Wrapping her arms around his neck, she stared up at him, marveling at how she'd managed to get this man. He was the love of her life.

She loved him more than anything else in the world. She didn't know how she could've doubted her feelings, not once could anyone have ever been good enough for her.

He captured her lips and she kissed him back,

sinking against him, moaning for more.

"You have no idea what you're doing to me, do you?" he said. "It's one of the many reasons why I love you."

"I love you too."

He took her lips again. She felt him reach down between them. His cock slid up and down her spread slit, and as he began to slowly push his cock inside her, she melted, wanting more.

"You have no idea how much I fucking love you, Robin. You're like a drug." He slammed his cock inside.

She wrapped her legs around him and groaned as he began rocking inside her.

He thrust all the way in, pulled out, and then slammed back in again. "Watch us."

She looked down at where they were joined. His cock throwing her deeper into pleasure. With each drive, it seemed to heighten her arousal. As he fucked her harder, making her take every single inch, she couldn't think. Who would want to?

He captured her hands, pressing them into the bed and fucking her even harder. "Come on, baby, I want to fuck you so damn bad. I've got a lot of time to make up for."

"Then fuck me, Preacher, make me your woman."

"You are my woman." He growled the words against her neck and she cried out, wanting more from him.

He drove into her and their fucking was a frenzy, but she didn't care. Making love and taking things slow could happen later. For now, all she wanted was to feel him. Every single part of him, and to never let him go, to bask in his touch. Needing more. He drove inside her, fucking her harder. As he came, she stared into his eyes, knowing there was nowhere else she'd rather be than with this man.

"I want to marry you," she said.

"I told you I didn't want to know the answer."

"I don't care. I love you. I want to be with you, and I think deep down, you want to be with me as well."

"You know me so well." He kissed her hard, and she closed her eyes, smiling. This was what it was all about. They'd been through hell to get to this moment and there was no way she was trading this for the world.

Wrapping her arms around him, she held him close as he kissed her neck. There was no way she would ever let him go, not again.

Reaper, she'd never loved him, not really. He'd been a means to an end, but now, it was about her and Preacher, and it would always be.

Chapter Eleven

Her time with Reaper

Staring down at the hotel floor, Robin tried not to think about him. She was pregnant, but she wasn't showing any signs of it yet. It wouldn't be too long before she did, though. It was getting harder. When she wasn't pregnant, being with Reaper was easier. He didn't remind her of Preacher, but a pregnancy? Having a baby? How could that not make her feel ... something?

She'd been pregnant with Preacher's baby, and now she was pregnant with Reaper's baby.

Her vision blurred as she thought about Preacher. It was easier to not think about him. To not take the time to even remember the loss. She was with Reaper now. She had to do whatever it took to survive.

Preacher was gone to her but right now, she knew she would never be able to remove his love. She loved him more than anything in the world and couldn't stop the feelings rushing through her body at the thought of not being with him.

She sniffled again and felt a little sick, but she ignored it. All she had to do right now was ignore the pain and all the feelings.

The door opened and she looked up to see Reaper smiling. If he knew why she was crying, he'd go a bit crazy.

It was all about survival. That was what she had to do. Survive.

"Morning," she said.

"I've got you breakfast." He held up a bag for her and she forced a smile to her lips.

"Have you been crying?"

"No. I'm fine. I'm just hungry. Starving even."

He moved toward her and as he wrapped his arms

around her, she wanted to push him away. She wanted to kick him, scream, hurt, kill, but instead, she pushed all of those feelings down, locking them up tight so no one could find them. No one could see them, and she could just go about her day without a single care in the world.

He kissed her head.

He didn't seem as happy to see her, but rather than dwell on that, she dug into her food, forcing herself to be happy. This was what she had to do. Be happy. She could do this for now, but she didn't know if she could do it for the rest of her life.

****

Present day

The days turned to weeks, and before Robin knew it, she was nearly four months pregnant, and Christmas was around the corner. She and Preacher had enjoyed Thanksgiving with Bethany.

Life, however strange, was slowly getting back to normal, or at least, their way of normal.

Running fingers through her hair, she looked out of the library window and saw Bishop walking across the road. After a quick glance inside, she saw Anne dealing with customers at the front desk, and wrapping her cardigan around her, she rushed out.

"Bishop," she said.

He stopped the moment she called his name, and she ran toward him.

"Hey."

"Hey, you."

Preacher had told her he hadn't known what to do with his son. He was at an impasse, and in truth, she didn't know what to do either. It was all a little confusing to her.

Licking her dry lips, she glanced around. It had started to snow.

"You love this time of year," he said.

"Yeah, I do." She didn't know what to say to him.

"It's hard, isn't it?" he asked. "Having a lot of history between us."

"I wanted you to die," she said. Her stomach twisted as she revealed the truth of some of her darker thoughts.

"I guess I should've expected that."

"I know it's wrong of me to think that, but I did. I thought about it a lot." She didn't know why she was telling him all of this. It wasn't like he had a right to know and yet here she was, telling him the truth when she didn't think she'd ever be able to be in his company ever again. They were both so different now. So much had passed between them. Neither of them were the same person.

"I get it."

"No, I don't think you do. You … you were my best friend and I couldn't believe you would do something so cold and yet, you did, without even caring about how it would affect me."

"I think it's safe to say, Robin, I wasn't a very nice guy. You think a day doesn't go by when I don't think about what I lost?" He laughed. "Look at me. I work at a feed store and a DIY place. I'm actually happy to be doing what I do, but it's not who I really am. You know me. You know what I'm capable of. My place should have been with my dad. I should've been learning everything from him. Right now, I'm waiting. That's all I've been doing for the past couple of months. I'm waiting for whatever punishment they're going to give to me, and then if I live, I'm going to try to make a life for myself. I know people here are afraid to get to know me again. I deserve all of this, and I deserve your hatred as well."

A MONSTER'S BEAUTY

"I don't hate you anymore." She sniffled. "I don't think we'll ever be best friends again. I believe that ship has long sailed, but I do want to be your friend, always," she said.

"Robin, I don't know. I can't ... I shouldn't."

"Please. A lot is happening in my life right now." She put a hand to her stomach.

"I wish you and my dad a very happy future." Bishop shoved his hands into his pockets. "I've got to get going. I've got to make some deliveries." He took a step away from her only to stop, turn, and then hug her tightly. "I'm so fucking sorry for everything. If I could, I'd change it. I hope you know that."

"Thank you." She watched him go after he pulled away from her. As he did, all she wanted to do was cry. So much had been lost and wasted.

Due to Bishop's petty jealousy, there was no real way of them ever getting their friendship back, and in truth, she didn't know if she really wanted to.

Turning back to the library, she saw Anne waiting for her.

"You do know you could get sick by being out in the cold."

"I'll be okay."

"You've got a death wish. You must have."

"No, no death wish from me." She sighed. "Do you think it's possible for people to become friends again even when they've put them through hell, or are the cause of that hell?"

"I honestly don't know. Basing it on Elijah and myself, it's not possible. Not even close. Anything else, I'm not sure." Anne put a comforting arm on her shoulder. "Tell me how everything is going with Preacher."

"You know how everything is going with

Preacher. He's the kind of guy who…" She looked down at her finger. He wanted to marry her the moment she gave birth.

Her nerves about the birth hadn't dissipated. If anything, they had gotten worse because she truly didn't know what to expect. They were both floating into uncharted territory. To help with her nerves, Randall had agreed to extra visits. He wouldn't do anything to harm the baby, but just to listen to her worries and concerns, which was more than she could have ever asked for.

Running fingers through her hair, she tried not to think about what had been going on in her life. So much had happened in what felt like a short space of time, but she knew it wasn't even close. Taking a deep breath, she tried not to think too hard.

"He's the kind of guy who…?"

"You know, he's just a hands-on kind of person. Nothing will ever get past him." She rolled her eyes. "I can't even believe I'm talking about this with you." She laughed. "This is all so crazy."

"Of course it is. Life is crazy."

"What is going on with you and Elijah?"

"The same old, same old. Only, he doesn't like that I might be seeing someone."

"Seriously?" Robin had an idea that the person she was seeing was, in fact, her father but she didn't say anything.

"Yeah."

"And is this thing with the other guy serious?"

"I don't know. I mean, there are times that it feels like it is going somewhere, you know, but then I've been so far out of the loop, I wouldn't even know what was up or down most days of the week. Elijah doesn't know him. He knows I'm seeing someone. We have separate rooms now. The kids, I don't know if us staying together is hurting them or not. The rumors suck, they always will." Anne blew out a breath. "Enough about me. Let's talk about you."

"There's nothing to talk about. The baby is fine. Preacher and I, we're fine. We're all fine. You know. No biggie."

"Then why are you nervous?"

"I guess I'm waiting for something bad to happen, you know? It's hard not to worry about the next thing. I can't help but wonder. It's fine. Ignore me."

"It's hard not to worry when you're talking like this."

She laughed. "I'm sorry. You're right about everything of course. Ignore me."

"No, I'm not saying don't talk about it. Just tell me."

They walked back behind the counter and Robin looked around the library. "I'm scared to be happy."

"Because of everything else that has happened?"

"Yes. Shouldn't I be afraid?" she asked. "The last time I was pregnant with Preacher's baby, I couldn't … it didn't last."

"I think you're worrying about all the wrong things."

"I don't know. Between losing my memory, being kidnapped, marrying a guy who I wasn't in fact married to. It's kind of hard to let yourself be free, to not worry about what's around the corner. I'm starting to think people like me don't get happy endings."

"Okay, now I need to know. People like you?"

"Yeah, I clearly have done something wrong, don't you think? In the past, or in something. I don't know. I just feel like I fucked up big time and now I'm being punished for it."

"I hate to say this, but you're starting to sound

like a crazy person. There's no rule book, Robin. There's no balance or something like that."

"Karma?"

"I personally don't believe in karma. For me, karma is just a thing people say and they don't even have to mean it. I could say that what I'm doing to Elijah is karma but I'm not going to give him that kind of power and you shouldn't be giving anyone karma either."

"You're right. I'm sorry. I just, I think I've been having a bad couple of days, and you're right. I shouldn't let fears get in the way."

"It's good to be worried, and to make sure everything is fine. I get that, and I even believe in that, but everything else, you need to let things go."

"I forgave Bishop." She pointed behind her, even though it was in the completely wrong direction. "That's a step forward, right?"

Anne laughed. "I wasn't thinking about him, but I guess in a way, yes, he's the same. You need to stop worrying. It's only going to make you feel sick." Anne put a comforting hand on her arm. "Now, you've got to learn to take care of yourself and to not worry about all that has happened before. This is about you and Preacher. Your little girl, and the baby you're due to give birth to. There's no right or wrong, here, just you and your feelings. Have your feelings changed about Preacher?"

"No."

"Then please stop worrying. You have nothing to worry about, I promise."

****

Preacher pulled Robin onto his lap and wrapped his arms around her, holding her close. "Do you want to tell me what's bothering you?"

Robin spent a great deal of time with him at the clubhouse lately. It helped that Bethany loved to play in his office, and he hadn't admitted his feelings to Robin yet, but he was totally loving the kid.

"I spoke to Bishop today," she said.

"Yeah, he's working hard, or at least that's what I've heard," he said.

"Yeah, he certainly seems to be. I guess it was a bit of a shock seeing him like that, you know? Carrying stuff. Being the big, strong guy. I think I'm used to him using his reputation with you." Robin leaned her head back. "He said he's waiting to know what it is you're going to do with him."

"Me?"

"Yeah. After everything that happened. He's waiting for you to either judge him or let him go."

"What did you say to him?"

"I didn't know what to say to him," she said. "There's a lot I don't know and I'm not privy to club business. I'm just a woman."

He cupped her face and tilted her head back, staring into her eyes. "I love you and whatever you have to say to me, even about the club, say it to me."

"Really? You won't be mad?"

"No, I won't be."

"Have you made a decision yet about Bishop?"

"Not as of yet, but that doesn't mean I won't make one. It can happen any time."

She took a deep breath. "Okay."

"Should I be worried?"

"I don't think you should kill him."

"You don't?"

"No. I think he needs to be able to live a long and happy life. One where he's not plagued by us, or what we do. I know it's asking a lot."

"It is asking a lot."

"And I'm sorry. I'm not sorry. I know this is a

club decision but we need to allow him to breathe."

"Is that what you want?" he asked.

"Yes."

"Then that's what I'll do, no questions asked. I'll talk to the club." He already knew the boys wanted to settle the problem with Bishop and he'd been putting it off as he had other dealings that took priority.

"I also want us to get married," Robin said. "Sooner rather than later. "I know you wanted to wait but I don't want to wait anymore. I think it's time we start to live our lives, don't you think?"

"You're all for the demands today. I don't get it. What changed?"

"Don't you think life is incredibly short?" she asked. "Look what has happened to us in the past couple of years. We've found each other, lost one another, and found each other again. I don't want to waste another moment. The only time my life makes any kind of sense is when I'm with you. I love you. No one else. Just you. You mean everything to me."

He stared into her eyes, and he saw the real worry, the real concern, and he couldn't bear for her to ever feel that way, not with him.

"Then I'll arrange it. You and me, we'll get married and I'll deal with Bishop. You have nothing to worry about."

"You're not mad?"

"No, why would I be mad?"

"I feel like I'm ruining all of your plans."

"Not a chance." He tilted her head back, kissed her lips. "I love you. I promise, I love you more than anything else in the world." Bethany began to giggle as she played with one of her toys. "In fact, there was something I wanted to talk to you about." He turned Robin so she was facing him and he smiled up at her.

"What is it?"

"I want to adopt Bethany. I want her to be my child."

"You would do that?" she asked.

"For you, I would do anything and I know that now. Don't go telling anyone just what a great guy I am. I've got to keep my reputation intact, you know."

"I'm speechless. I don't know what to say."

"Say yes, and make me really happy."

"Yes."

"Good." He gripped the back of her head and kissed her hard. "I love you."

"And I love you."

****

A couple of days later, Preacher went to Bishop's apartment. He'd known where the kid was living for some time now. Not only had Bishop gotten a job but he'd been getting on his own two feet, and he was proud.

Lifting his hand, he knocked on the door and waited. He'd gone to the feed and DIY store to discover his son spent a great deal of his time here.

He waited.

Bishop flicked the catch of the lock and opened the door.

"Preacher," he said.

"Son."

"What brings you here?"

"You know what brings me here and I think it's time you and I had a talk."

He watched his son visibly swallow but stepped back, giving him plenty of room to enter. Glancing around the place, he was surprised to see it was tidy. "You know the women at the club were afraid to clean your room. Lots of dirty dishes and unwashed clothes."

"Yeah, well, back then I felt I was a fucking king

and now I know I'm not. The only person I can rely on is myself." Bishop closed the door, folding his arms. "What can I do for you?"

"Simple, really, the club has made a decision." It had been a unanimous decision. Preacher hadn't even had to persuade any of the men to let his son go. They had all agreed Bishop was owed some slack for all of his time and effort he'd put into the club, at least to right the wrong that had been done to them.

Without Bishop, he would have struggled to find the Slaves to the Beasts' place of rest. Reaper was good at hiding, and he'd made sure all of his men at the club were just as good.

Bishop nodded his head. "I'm ready. Whatever that might be." He held his hand up. "Wait. I … yeah, I'm ready."

"You're sure?"

"No, I want to get something off my chest first. Before I don't have a chance or whatever. I hated you. For the longest time, I hated the kind of power you had. All you had to do was click your fingers and people came running. Everyone was always afraid of you."

"And you didn't like that."

"I was only ever going to be your son. Your boy. I hated it, but now I realize I should've respected it. Because of you, I did have a good life. Don't get me wrong, you were a shitty father, but what you were like with me is in no way what you were like with anyone else, Robin included."

He ran a hand down his face. "I messed up with her, big time. I did and said shit I shouldn't have done. My biggest failure was not helping her when Reaper came calling. I was a monster and I shouldn't have done what I did. Not only did I let him take her, but I made sure he knew when you were coming. I always kept him one step ahead. Each time, I hated myself for it, but after a while, I was too afraid to tell you the truth, so I kept it from you. That was wrong of me, and I am sorry. So sorry. I wish I could change what I did, and now, I don't think I can ever put it right. I hope you and Robin not only have a healthy baby, but I also hope you're happy. I won't do anything to hurt you or Robin ever again."

Bishop nodded his head. "Right, I've said what I needed to say. I hope you can believe me."

"I do believe you," Preacher said. "The club isn't going to punish you. You'll never be allowed to become a member, and you'll be an outsider. You won't be privy to ever becoming a prospect or joining. The women are not allowed to sleep with you. You can stay in town, or leave, it's up to you. You're a free man without a mark on your head."

"Wait? What?"

"You're a free man."

"No, that's not possible, not after everything I've done."

"You've done nothing wrong. You are free to go." Preacher stared at his son. "I think it's safe to say you were never meant for this life, Bishop. You've got your own life to lead, your own path to follow, and it doesn't include me."

"I'd ... I would like to stay. I want to be able to make it up to you and to Robin."

"You will stay away from Robin unless she wills it. You are not to go near her, do you understand?"

"Yes."

Preacher nodded. "So long as we're in agreement, then it doesn't matter. I'll leave you, and Merry Christmas." He walked toward the door.

"I'm sorry, Dad. I know nothing I say can make up for what I did."

Preacher spun back to look at his son. "I want to make one thing clear right now. The club has voted for you to be free. I agree with their decision but between me and you, I will never forgive you. Robin told me she has forgiven you, but I don't have that kind of strength. I see you, Bishop, and what I see, I really don't like."

Preacher looked at his boy. "I fucked up with you, I know that, but that was between me and you. Instead of you taking your anger and hatred out on me, you didn't, you took it out on the woman I love. She cared about you at some point as well. She can forgive you, but I never will. I won't seek you out. I won't harm you, but this is my final warning to you, son. If you ever intend to hurt the woman I love, my family, or my club, I will end you."

"I won't." Bishop held his hands up. "You've given me more than my fair chance. I'm sorry for everything I've done."

Preacher wanted to say more, but instead, he left the apartment. There was nothing more that could be said. All the words that needed to be spoken had been. They were done now. Whatever debt or guilt he owed to Bishop was done. His men were more than willing to allow him to live, especially after he had helped them. It was all they were willing to do. Bishop would have a complete ban from all of the club activities and from ever being part of it.

His son was dead to him as far as the club went. Preacher knew on a personal level, he had a great hatred for his son. The two years Robin was taken from him, he was never ever going to get them back. He could hold a grudge for as long as he needed to, no questions asked. When it came to Bishop, he had no lost feelings, no upset, just an understanding that his son meant nothing to him.

A MONSTER'S BEAUTY

After leaving his apartment, he made his way toward the town's library. Robin was determined to work and study there. It was the perfect place for her to keep an eye on Bethany as well. When he entered, several kids were leaving and they all gave him a wide berth.

All the rumors of what a monster he was still circulated, and he had no interest in changing anyone's mind.

He found Anne working at the counter. She held Bethany on her hip and the moment his girl saw him, she started to wave her hands excitedly. It was moments like this that he couldn't do anything wrong to this child. She was a complete innocent in all of this, and he would love her as his own.

"Here you go, I think she wants you," Anne said. Bethany was holding out her arms toward him, and he took her.

"Where's my other girl?"

"She's studying. I know she wants to graduate now before the baby comes and I think it's important to her, so I've forced her to take some rest and given her space."

"I'll pay you for all the time she's taken here."

"You don't need to do that."

"I want to."

"Have you heard from Bear lately?"

"Yeah, he's around. Why?"

"No reason."

He raised a brow.

"Don't look at me like that. There is a reason, but it's private."

"I'll let him know you're looking for him."

"Thank you. I need him to talk to me."

"You worry way too much."

"I worry enough." She ran fingers through her

hair. "Do you want me to take her?"

"Nah, I've got her." He walked in the direction where Anne pointed and he found Robin, asleep on top of a table filled with books. She worried way too much and it was showing now.

With their girl on his hip, he pulled the chair out closest to her, and as he sat down, she woke up.

"Oh, no, is it late? Where am I? What am I doing?" Robin asked.

"It's a little after twelve. You're at the library. You were sleeping and I imagine before that you were studying."

She groaned. "I only closed my eyes for a minute."

"Why is it so important for you to graduate before our baby comes?" he asked.

"I don't know. It just is. I think … I'm scared. I'm not going to have time to study when the baby comes. I remember what it was like with Bethany." She reached out, stroking their girl's cheek. She was already curling up in Preacher's arms getting ready to go to sleep.

"You're doing too much and when you do, it tires you out."

"I know. I know."

"Do I have to bribe Randall to put you on bed rest?"

"You shouldn't be able to bribe anyone," she said.

"This is me you're talking to."

"Yeah, yeah, I know. I just, I want this, you know. I feel like I'm finally getting my life back and if I can do this, then I'm not failing? It probably makes no sense."

"It makes a lot of sense. More sense than you

even realize."

She blew out a breath as her stomach started to growl. "What do I owe the social call to?"

"I talked to Bishop. A decision has been made." He watched her tense.

"It has? That was fast."

He laughed. "You think that's fast?"

"You know what I mean."

"He's going to be free."

"Free?"

"Yeah. The guys took into account his help during the ... well, Reaper, and he can never join the club or have any association. On that score, he's well and truly finished."

"Wow. This is certainly a morning to remember. I mean, did you do this?"

"Robin, I want to be clear on something." He reached for her hand, the one carrying his engagement ring. "I'm not a good man. I will never claim to be anything of the sort. I won't even sit here and pretend I in some way stopped the boys from making the right decision. It's not who I am, and it never will be."

He ran his thumb across the tiny diamond. He'd spent a small fortune on it and seeing it on her finger gave him a thrill. "I'm going to be honest with you, I want to kill Bishop."

"He's your son."

"And he fucked up big time. I can't just forgive shit like that. It's not who I am."

"Then who is it?" she asked. "I don't want you to kill Bishop because of me. There's already a lot of death on my hands."

"No. It's not." He squeezed her hand, hoping to offer her some comfort, but she shook her head.

"Yes, it is. Milly. O'Klaren. My mom. Reaper.

His club. It's all because of me." She started to have tears in her eyes. "How can I not be filled with so much regret? If I'd died, none of this would have happened."

Preacher gritted his teeth. "Let me be clear and I will only ever say this once, and you will never bring it up. Milly died because she hurt you. Not only did she drug you, she put you in a bad situation. It could have been a lot worse. She disobeyed the club. O'Klaren, that fucker took everything from us. He had it coming. I will never mourn his death. Your mother, she was in bed with him. She wanted you to suffer, and in no way should you feel sorry for her. She was a spiteful bitch with a rotten cunt. Don't ever regret her death. She would've done everything in her power to make you suffer. Reaper and his club. I know you had feelings for him. I don't want to understand it, but what makes everything worse is that I do. The only good thing to come from your time with him is this little girl, and believe me, she is a very special, beautiful girl. Now, I love you. You will not feel guilt or pain, or any other kinds of those feelings. Do you understand me?"

"I understand."

"No buts. Nothing. Your hands are clean. They will always be clean and I promise you, Robin, I'm going to make sure you never know pain or death again." He gripped the back of her neck and pulled her closer. "Now, I hate to be the bearer of bad news but this kid has taken a big dump and it stinks. I don't do diapers."

Robin burst out laughing as she wiped away the tears.

A MONSTER'S BEAUTY

Chapter Twelve

"You both look nervous," Randall said.

Robin held Preacher's hand, feeling a little sick. "Not nervous. Our baby has been, you know, a little evasive."

"You do know in some cases the sex of the baby is never confirmed until birth. I can't give you an answer if the little guy or girl doesn't want me to see." Randall sat on the chair beside her, clicking on the monitor in front of him.

"I get it." She turned to Preacher. "We want to know if it's a boy or girl."

"So long as it will let us."

"It?" Robin asked.

"What? I don't know what else to call … that thing."

"Seriously. Our baby, our child, baby, any kind of reference to our child being someone rather than an *it*."

"You're taking it a little too personally. I think her hormones are all out of whack, Doctor," Preacher said.

"He blames everything on the hormones. I no longer enjoy chocolate pancakes and it's all because of my hormones. I swear if I didn't like him one day, he'd blame the baby."

"Probably."

Randall chuckled. "It's good to see you two like this. I did worry you wouldn't be able to work out your differences, but now I see you're both giving each other a real chance. Now, this gel will be a little cold. We've gone through this before."

She nodded. It was cold on her stomach. She took a deep breath and then she heard the beautiful sound of a heartbeat.

"Good and strong, I like that. So I hear you two will be getting married in a couple of weeks," Randall said.

"We're having a small ceremony at the clubhouse," Robin said.

"To which you're invited, if you'd like," Preacher asked.

"I did wonder. I've yet to receive my invitation in the mail."

"We didn't send any out, so you'd be waiting. We knew we were coming to see you, and so we waited to invite you in person," Robin said. "Of course if you'd like to come, that is."

"I would love to. It would be nice to see you both happy and settling down. Why the clubhouse? Why not in a church?" Randall asked.

Robin looked at her fiancé. He'd been the one to suggest the church. "I didn't want to get married in a church. I feel our life together began at the clubhouse and that's where we should be united." She smiled at him. "Where did you and your wife have your ceremony?"

"Ah, we had it the good old traditional way. Lots of family. Lots of expectation."

"Did you hate it?"

"Loathed it. Couldn't stand it. Never wanted to do any of it, but I didn't have much choice. I loved my woman, and she's the one I would go to the ends of the earth for. There will always be someone out there for you."

"You believe that?" Preacher asked.

"Tell me what you think when you look at your woman. There's no one else like her. You'll do anything for her. It's how life is supposed to be, and I refuse to believe in anything different. Now, let's see if we can get this little one to show us what they are."

Robin felt Preacher's lips on her hand. She couldn't have been happier. The dress she intended to wear was already picked out. It was one she'd been wanting since she was young.

"We have an answer," Randall said. "Do you both still want to know?"

"Yes," they said in unison.

Randall did some more typing on the computer and spun the monitor around for them to see.

"You are both looking at your beautiful, healthy baby boy."

Tears filled her eyes. The image wasn't clear, but she knew it was their baby.

"A baby brother for Bethany. I love you."

She thought about Bishop but pushed any fears aside. She wasn't Bishop's mother. She still saw her friend around town, but everything was different now.

"So, I expect you to rest. Get married, have more rest, and be ready. Boys can be quite a handful," Randall said. "Do you have any questions for me?"

"None," she said.

"Nothing," Preacher said. He opened his jacket and pulled out some money. Randall took it, handing them back a picture of their son, and they left the office, heading out to the waiting car. She couldn't go on his bike until after the baby was born. Preacher opened the door for her. She climbed inside and stared down at the ultrasound picture.

"You know, I didn't get one for Bethany. Reaper was too worried in case it left a paper trail. He would never allow me to keep on."

"The man was an asshole, but he was probably right. Most paper trails can be followed."

She glanced over at him. His knuckles were white as he gripped the steering wheel. "So, a healthy boy."

"Yep."

She didn't like his curt response. Nibbling on her lip, she tried to think of something more to say but came up blank. "Er, I don't know what else to say."

"There's nothing more to say."

"Preacher, what's going on?"

"Nothing."

"You're acting different. I don't understand why."

"There's nothing to talk about," he said. "Nothing at all."

She stared straight ahead and nerves ate away at her. Why was he closing off from her? She didn't understand it, nor did she like it. This wasn't Preacher at all.

"I don't understand what's going on. Don't even think about lying to me. Is this all a little too real for you now? Do you not want to marry me?"

"Don't even think that."

"Then what am I supposed to think? I don't know what's going on in that head of yours, do I? I don't know what you want from me. We're going to have a healthy, beautiful baby boy."

"I heard."

"Why are you angry?"

"Look what happened to the last son I had, huh? Look what I did to him. You know what, I don't want to fucking deal with this right now. I'm not getting into this with you. Fuck it."

"Please, Preacher, you're not making any sense to me. This has nothing to do with Bishop."

"It has everything to do with Bishop."

"How?" She frowned, so confused. "We've had good news."

"I wanted a little girl."

"We've got a little girl."

"I'm not... I'm not a good father, Robin. Can't you see that? I've never been a good father."

"You're perfect with Bethany."

"Yeah, because ... I don't fucking know why I'm good with her, but look what I did to Bishop. I fucked him up in ways I didn't think was possible. I'm not a good man and you think I am."

"Preacher, I have no expectations of you."

"I'm going to ruin our child's life. I just know I am."

"He's not even born yet."

"You know what I mean," he said.

"I don't. I don't have a clue why you're so afraid. He's going to be our son, and we will raise him together."

"I don't know what it means to be a good father."

"Do you really think anyone in this world knows what it means to be good at anything?"

"I'm not talking about the world. I'm talking about me."

"And I'm trying to get you to see that your fears are like every other man's. You're not the only person in the world who's afraid of fucking up. We all are." The tears she'd tried so hard to keep contained spilled down her cheeks.

"You think this is easy for me? I have one daughter who I forgot for nearly a year. I had no recollection of Bethany. I mean, wow, I saw her, touched her cheek in the supermarket, and I still didn't recognize her. Yet, talking to me now, I wouldn't think there was any way I wouldn't be able to know my child. We can't be held accountable for everything, Preacher."

"I'm a bad fucking father and that's all you need to know. This son of ours, it's a mistake."

She took his hand and placed it across her chest. "You think this is a mistake, but I say you're so damn wrong. There's no mistake when we love each other the way we do. I love you more than anything else in the world, and I will fight for you every single time, Preacher. This hasn't been easy. I don't expect it is, but if you're basing it on Bishop and what happened to you by your own father, then you are wrong. We'll get through this together. We are new parents and if we can love and take care of Bethany, then no matter the sex of our child, we will love our baby no matter what. You will be the perfect dad. We'll help each other be perfect for one another. I know this is going to be long and scary but together, we can do this."

"You think so?"

Robin couldn't recall ever seeing him so vulnerable. Cupping his face, she pulled him close and kissed his mouth. "Yes, I do. We've been through so much together and I have faith in you, in us. I know we can make this work, and we're going to make this work. Trust in me. Trust in us."

He stroked her cheek. "I don't know how it happened, but falling for you was the best fucking thing I ever did."

He kissed her hard, and Robin felt it all the way down into her core. She wouldn't give up on him, on them. She would fight for him with every single fiber of her being.

****

"Do you want to make a run for it?" Bear asked one month later.

"Shut up."

"I'm just saying. It's the clubhouse and if anyone has a way out of here, it's you."

"Shut up."

A MONSTER'S BEAUTY

"I know Robin's my daughter and she could totally do with a better man than you. You know, between the titty clubs, the pussy you own, drugs, guns, fights, the blood on your hands. I should be dragging my daughter back home and telling her to never leave the house. That's what a good father would have done."

"Are you done?"

"Not quite. I have to make sure you're ready, to, you know, stick the course with my girl."

"I love your girl. I always will."

Bear smiled. "Good."

"I won't do anything to harm her."

"She's taking so long. Do you think she ran off?"

"No. Robin wants this day to be perfect." He also knew after a long phone call last night that she was worried about how she would look in a white gown swollen with his kid. Like he told her, it didn't matter what she looked like to him. He would love her regardless. They had come this far and her pregnant state wouldn't turn him off, it would do the very fucking opposite.

Running fingers through his hair, he felt his body go on high alert. Dog was in residence. Preacher had decided at the last minute to invite the leader and he'd brought a couple of his men with him, even though this was a day for peace. He didn't mind. Anyone would be fucking foolish to enter a situation like this which could be a trap.

"So this is what a wedding looks like," Dog said.

"You're supposed to take a seat."

"Oh, I will when I'm ready. Do women want this?"

"Not all the time but Robin's special."

"I'd say. You've gone to the ends of the earth for this woman, and you've done so without caring who you take down in the process. Robin is a very special woman. I doubt all women are this special."

"You've just got to meet the right one," Bear said.

At that precise moment, silence fell on the clubhouse garden. Preacher had paid good money to some decorators to have everything looking perfect for what Robin wanted. This was no church, but she would get close to it.

Bear cleared his throat and made his way down the aisle to assist his daughter. It was still his place to walk her down.

Dog, being well, Dog, took Bear's place.

"I always knew you'd want me as a best man."

"I didn't ask you."

"I know, but Bear gave me the rings so I could play my part. You don't see me as the kind of guy who will sit in with the crowd now, do you?"

"To be honest, I don't know what I fucking think anymore," he said. All he wanted was to marry his woman and live happily ever after for fucking once.

The music started up, and Robin came toward him. She wore white, as she should, and Preacher only had eyes for her. There was no other woman who would ever be there for him. Who he could ever love more.

Bear held her close before taking her hand and placing it inside Preacher's, and they stood together.

"You look beautiful."

"So do you."

"I was going more for devilishly handsome." He winked at her.

"I was thinking more hot, sexy biker, but I like it. I'm going for the whale look." She put a hand on her stomach. "You think I pull it off?"

"No, you don't. You pull off Preacher's woman a

hell of a lot better."

The priest cleared his throat and Preacher listened with half an ear. He was too busy watching his woman and how admiring how stunning she looked. Everything about her would soon belong to him, and he couldn't fucking wait to claim her. Every last part of her.

They both spoke their vows, promising to love, honor, and respect each other. Those were the vows they wrote for each other. When the time came to kiss the bride, Preacher had never been more impatient to do so. The moment he did, the crowd went nuts. The priest stayed for as long as he was able.

Beer was already flowing, the music blasting on high.

Anne rushed toward her and hugged her close. "I'm so happy for you. For both of you."

"Thank you."

"You'll treat my girl right?"

"I will treat her the best way possible." Preacher gripped the back of her neck, tilting her back so he could kiss her. "Now, I think it's time I danced with my wife."

That would be something he was going to have to get used to. His wife. *My wife.* It didn't matter how many times he said it, it still seemed surreal.

He took Robin in his arms as it didn't matter where he danced with her, only that she was in his arms, his wife, his everything.

"How are you feeling?" he asked.

"I can't believe we're married. It seems like all of this is happening to someone else."

Anne was taking care of Bethany with Bear's help. Bear had finally decided to come around to having a grandkid and was making up for lost time. Meanwhile, he knew Anne was looking for a way to divorce Elijah. She'd come to him for help but asked for him to keep it quiet until she knew more. What she didn't want was for Elijah to do something crazy or insane.

With his wife in his hands, Preacher didn't let her go. Not even when Bear and Dog wanted to dance with her. He simply held her close, refusing to give her a chance to go.

They enjoyed some cake, listened to a couple of bad speeches, and finally, by the end of the night, Preacher was able to take her home.

He took her back to their home, picked her up in his arms, and carried her over the threshold. He made her keep her arms tight around his neck as he locked the door, wanting no interruptions. He took her to the stairs, and then up to their bedroom, where he placed her gently on the bed. Tucking some hair back from her ear, he smiled down at her. She gripped his face and kissed him hard. They both held each other tightly, and he didn't want to let her go.

"There's something I want you to know." He dropped her hands off him.

"Preacher?"

He moved to the closet and removed his jacket. He'd already folded it up and he moved toward the bed. "This is yours."

"I don't understand. This is your leather cut." She stroked her fingers over the patch marking it as his.

He took her hand. "I'm willing to give it all up. For you, for our son, for Bethany. I want us to have a good life. A life where you don't have to worry about every single knock. I can leave at any time. We can set up a new life together. The four of us."

She shook her head. "You want to do all of that for me?"

"I hope you realize exactly what I'm willing to do for you. Not a moment goes by when I don't think about all the things you could have and what I want you to have."

"Preacher, I … no," she said. "This is your cut. This is your life. I didn't marry you for you to walk away from this. This is who you are and I accept and love you for you. Not for some cut, or some patch." She went to her knees before him. "You're so going to have to help me up."

He chuckled. "I will. I want you to know exactly how I feel about you. What you mean to me."

Tears were in her eyes, spilling down her cheeks. "You know, I think I'm starting to get it." She put her hand on his heart. "I'm here, aren't I? No one else has ever gotten so close to you, but this heart, it belongs to me."

"I'm all yours, Robin. Every single part of me is yours." He kissed her hard and she moaned.

"Then I'm all yours, and I love every single part of you, even the bits I struggle with. You're the president of the Twisted Monsters MC. I'm your wife, and I will be by your side, no matter what we face. I never stopped loving you, Preacher, and guess what? I never, ever will."

He lifted her to her feet and stripped the wedding dress off her, well, tore it off. It was all pretty fabric that got in his way, and he wasn't interested in anything being in his way as he made love to his wife.

After placing her on the bed, he settled between her spread thighs, licking at her sweet pussy, tasting her cunt on his tongue. Only when she was screaming at him for more did he finally fuck her, taking her, making her his wife, his woman, his soulmate, for the rest of his life, and he intended to make the rest of her life so incredibly happy. He had a lot of time now to get it right, and right he would.

Epilogue One

"I hate you," Robin said, screaming as a wave of pain washed over her.

"I know, baby. You can keep on hating me for a long time as well. It's not going to change the fact we're here and now. I will love you and hold you for the rest of my life. Come on, baby, push. You can do it. Keep on pushing."

She released a scream as Preacher and Randall both encouraged her to push. This baby was going to be the death of her. She knew it. There was no way he wasn't going to be. He was already late and it would seem her little boy didn't want to come out.

Collapsing to the bed, she moaned. "I can't do anymore."

"We're nearly there, Robin. Come on, you can do this," Randall said.

Preacher was there, holding her hand. "I've got you. I'm not going to let you go. I need you. We're doing this together."

"No, we did this together, but everything else," she said, sniffling. "It's not right. I'm not ready."

"Come on, baby."

"It hurts."

"Not much longer."

Her impatience was starting to grow now. She wanted to see her son, to feel him against her, and as she lifted up, screamed, and bore down, she didn't give up, she didn't admit defeat.

Preacher held her hand as she bore down, her cries of pain and agony filled the air, and not being able to stop it. When her baby finally came out, he did so with a cry, and it was the most precious sound in the world.

The doctors and nurses took him to do their

necessary measurements as Robin collapsed to the bed again. Only this time, she didn't have to get back up. She could fall asleep. Her job was done.

"Fuck me, baby, you're strong. You're amazing."

She smiled up at him. "We did it."

"Here you go," Randall said. "Here is your beautiful boy."

She held her arms open and took their boy. Preacher stroked his head lightly.

"He's so tiny."

"He'll grow, trust me," Randall said. "Have you picked a name yet?"

She looked at Preacher.

"We're naming him Caleb Junior, after myself," Preacher said.

"Interesting name. I'll leave you two."

"Hello, Caleb. I'm your mommy. There's your daddy. We're going to love and hold you, and cherish you forever. You will be so loved."

"I love you, Robin, so fucking much," Preacher said.

For one of the very few times in her life, she saw Preacher crying. "Don't cry."

"I'm not crying." He didn't make a move to wipe the tears away but she knew he felt a great deal and for that, she would cherish these moments for the rest of her life. Kissing the top of her boy's head, she hoped to have many more of these moments.

****

Six months later

"Do you have any idea how dangerous it could have been?" Preacher asked, holding his son in one arm as Bethany was also on his back.

Robin dropped the back of her shirt and turned toward him. She reached for Bethany, pulling their daughter into her arms.

"I wasn't going to have his name on my flesh anymore. We made a decision together, Preacher. I'm not his. I was never his, and I'm not going to wear his mark as any kind of proof or attachment to him. I'm done. I love you. I want you. That's final. Now, do you want to argue about this some more?" she asked. "I've got to take care of it. I've got the salve which you can rub in regularly. I've got some aftercare instructions. Believe me, nothing bad is going to come of it."

"I didn't think anything bad would come of it. I wanted to be there."

Seeing Reaper's name removed from her back was something he'd been looking forward to. Robin had come to him because she wanted it removed completely and he was more than willing to give his woman what she wanted, even if it meant he was going to have to wait to see that name gone.

Robin sighed. "You hate to see me in pain. Believe me, getting a tattoo is not easy for me. I cry. I get all emotional and weepy. It's not pretty. I wasn't being selfish. I think I was trying to save the artist's life. This is for you, all of you. Every single part of me is yours. I would have had it done sooner if I could. Please don't be mad at me."

Just then, Caleb Junior chose that moment to start screaming and Bethany laughed. "She has a sick sense of humor," he said, smiling. He loved to hear his daughter laugh.

"I better feed him." They swapped children and Bethany started to play with his patches on his jacket.

"You're not mad anymore, are you?"

"No, I'm not mad."

"Good. I don't want you to be mad." She cupped his cheek. "I love you."

A MONSTER'S BEAUTY

When the ink on the base of her back finally healed, he would see the name had been covered with a nice, deep red rose. Above it, his name was curved around the rose. The symbolism wasn't lost on him.

Epilogue Two

Fourteen years later

"You got sent home today for beating a kid to a bloody pulp."

"He deserved it," Caleb Junior said. "I wanted to kill him, but I didn't. I let him live."

"Do you want to tell me why you decided to beat a kid up?" Preacher sat on the end of his son's bed.

Caleb Junior was growing up so fast. Fourteen years old and not a day went by that he didn't worry about him, about any of his children. All five of them, six if he included Bishop.

His firstborn son had never left town. In fact, against all odds, he'd become the handyman to the town. If anyone needed a repair, Bishop became the most reliable, cost-effective guy. He'd been able to build a business and a family. Five years after Caleb Junior's birth, he and Bishop had a sit-down and were able in some way to mend the damage they had both caused. They'd never be close, Preacher knew that, and the truth was, he didn't want to be.

Bishop and Robin had also become good friends, or at least, she'd become good friends with his wife, but that was a whole other interesting development. For now, he was more interested in his younger son's very bad behavior.

"Look, there's this girl, okay?" Caleb said. His fourteen-year-old face started to go red.

"A girl?"

"Dad, please. It's not like that. She's different from others. He was calling her names. She has to wear braces and she's on the chubby side, and well, she's nice." Caleb shrugged. "Her parents moved here not that long ago and she's having a hard time at school. Benji is a prick."

"Don't let your mother catch you saying such things."

"He is though. A really big one. He's worse than any kind of pussy and he likes to hurt her. I don't like him and he was saying all kinds of bad things to her. But today he told her he was going to gut her and see what her insides look like. I know that's fucking weird."

"Language."

"And so I let him know that she would never be alone. That if he wants to ever, and I mean ever hurt her, he's going to have to come through me."

"So you're telling me you've been sent home because you like a girl and were defending her?"

"Yeah, that's exactly what I'm saying, but I don't like, like her *like her*. It's complicated."

"You should have told a teacher."

"But what if what he's saying is true?" Caleb Junior asked. "What if he would hurt her? Should I let it go?"

"No, you should have told a teacher. That's what people do, Caleb Junior."

"I'm not a normal person. I'm going to be like you one day, Dad. I'm going to run the club and no one's ever going to be able to threaten women again. I'll take care of them, like you do for Mom."

Preacher smiled. "First, you've got to find a woman you love as much as I love your mother." He sighed.

"Am I in trouble?"

"You've got homework. Your mother went back to the school and demanded you be given a chance. So she got you like a month's worth of homework."

"Man, that's so not fair."

"You'll do it for your mother though, right? So

she's not worried about you or your future?"

"I guess, but it's lame. I know she didn't get to graduate at first and everything, but she's like super smart."

Robin did eventually graduate after Caleb was born. She didn't stop there though. She went on to college where she could take courses online. She decided on English. Even though she had only ever been his wife and worked at the library, she continued her education, and he loved it when she debated with him.

Their conversations certainly turned down a dirtier route when they didn't agree.

"Don't speak like that in front of your mother and we'll call it a day."

"Okay, fine."

He chuckled. Leaving his son with some of the homework, he made his way downstairs to find his wife worrying.

"What did he say? Should we worry?" Robin asked.

In fourteen years of being married to each other, he didn't know how it was possible, but she had grown even more beautiful.

"Our son was doing the right thing for a girl. You would be so proud of him."

She breathed a sigh of relief. "Proud of him?"

"Yes. He's cursing like the best of us, but his heart is in the right place." He moved up toward his wife, holding her close as he listened to their house.

Bethany was in her room, studying. His little girl wanted to be a doctor and help every single person in the world. She had a plan to bring about world peace, one town at a time. He loved her so much.

Caleb Junior was now doing his homework, and it would seem he was falling in love at a young age.

A MONSTER'S BEAUTY

Abigail was probably playing with some cars. She didn't like what she considered *girls'* dolls and often showed her disappointment in being forced to buy them. She also hated long hair, and one morning they had woken to find she had cut it all off.

Neal was the one into sports. In the distance, he heard a game on the television. No sound from Neal, but he was there, absorbing all the knowledge.

Then of course was their young, sweet little Riley, asleep up in the nursery. The nursery that had once been a place of great sorrow that they'd been able to turn into a place of great love. A sign of them both coming together.

"Can you believe how quiet the house is?" Robin asked.

He wrapped his arms around her. Any other time, he would have tried to take her upstairs, but he'd learned his lesson.

He counted down.

Five.

Four.

Three.

Two.

One.

With five kids aged between fifteen and one, there was no way peace and quiet could last forever, and it didn't.

This was his life.

His love.

His passion.

And he wouldn't trade this life for anything.

The End

Note from Author

Thank you all so much for joining me for the journey that was Robin and Preacher's story. It has been a true passion of mine and I loved every second of writing it. As you can imagine, I will be doing more books in this series. I can tell you so far, Dog, Bear, and even Bishop will be getting a story but I think their books will be more of a standalone than a trilogy.

This is the end of my very first trilogy and I really hope you enjoyed it.

Book One: To Awaken a Monster

Book Two: Taken by a Monster

Book Three: A Monster's Beauty

www.samcrescent.com

A MONSTER'S BEAUTY

SAM CRESCENT

EVERNIGHT PUBLISHING ®

www.evernightpublishing.com